Enriching
the Curriculum
with Art Experiences

Early Childhood Education
providing lessons for life

www.EarlyChildEd.delmar.com

Enriching the Curriculum with Art Experiences

Wendy M. L. Libby

DELMAR

THOMSON LEARNING ™   Australia   Canada   Mexico   Singapore   Spain   United Kingdom   United States

DELMAR
THOMSON LEARNING™

Enriching the Curriculum with Art Experiences
by Wendy M. L. Libby

Business Unit Director:
Susan L. Simpfenderfer

Executive Editor:
Marlene McHugh Pratt

Acquisitions Editor:
Erin O'Connor Traylor

Editorial Assistant:
Alexis Ferraro

Executive Production Manager:
Wendy A. Troeger

Production Editor:
Elaine Scull

Executive Marketing Manager:
Donna J. Lewis

Channel Manager:
Nigar Hale

Cover Design:
Joseph Villanova

For permission to use material from this text or product, contact us by
Tel   (800) 730-2214
Fax   (800) 730-2215
www.thomsonrights.com

Library of Congress Cataloging-in-Publication Data

Libby, Wendy M. L.
  Enriching the curriculum with art experiences / by Wendy M. L. Libby.
      p.   cm.
  Includes bibliographical references.
  ISBN 0-7668-3833-1
    1. Art—Study and teaching (Primary)—United States.   2. Art—Study and teaching (Preschool)—United States.   3. Art in education—United States.   I. Title.
  N361 .L48 2002
  372.5'044—dc21

                                                        2001028796

NOTICE TO THE READER

To my husband, Bob, who is my partner in life; to my sons, Brandon and Bradley, who are my true creations; and to my Mom and Dad who are my guiding lights.

Contents

Contents

Preface

For twenty-three years, I have been an elementary art teacher in the Bangor School Department in the state of Maine. Over the years, my colleagues and I have worked to build a strong art department where visual expression is highly valued across the curriculum. Thanks to educational and community support, art is an integral part of my school system's curriculum.

All children are capable of creating. The realization that they can create is an important component of a positive self-concept. An adult's appreciation and acceptance play a valuable role in enhancing a child's self-esteem. By arranging colors, lines, and shapes, children can express ideas and feelings about themselves and the world. The visual expression then becomes an intellectual and emotional recording. Art helps children grow creatively, emotionally, socially, physically, intellectually, and aesthetically.

Because all children are unique and special in their own way, their artwork will be equally unique. It is important to communicate that there is no better or best in art, only variety, and that each child's work is worthy of the effort put forth. Building children's self-esteem causes their skills to improve as well, because they take pride in their efforts.

In making art, the process is more important than the product. Children need to gain control over the materials before they can arrange them creatively, in order to express themselves. Children should be encouraged to express their own feelings and to respond imaginatively. An expressive and enthusiastic teacher motivates children to be eager and excited about their work. The value of their creative expressions can be communicated by individual discussions and praise, with group sharing and evaluations, and by exhibiting the creative artwork when it is completed.

Motivating a child in art is a fairly easy task. For young children the major factor in motivation is the art material itself. Simply manipulating the medium is often stimulus enough. Possibilities for creation are discovered through experimentation. The presentation of visual stimuli also serves to intrigue children and challenge their creativity. Reproductions of artists' works, photographs, illustrations, actual objects, and field trips are a few that have positive appeal. In order to guide children in art, it is not necessary for teachers to have the know-how or talent to draw themselves, as many adults assume. Art does not require a single right answer. Rather, an art experience should be open-ended, with results that resolve in a variety of ways. This encourages divergent thinking and the generation of novel ideas.

Art in the curriculum is invaluable and creating images is indispensable. The visual thinking that art requires is an important factor for advancement in math and the sciences. Writing skills and language development are strengthened through observation, listening, questioning, and describing, all of which are important procedures in art experiences.

Although educators value the arts in the schools there are, unfortunately, many school systems that do not have an art teacher. With or without trained art teachers, classroom teachers should use art experiences and visuals to enhance their teaching of any subject in the curriculum. Although formal art training is not necessary, teachers should become familiar with the basics—art elements, art principles, art media, and art techniques—in order to implement art experiences and visuals in a meaningful and productive manner. This is the purpose of my writing this book.

As a workshop facilitator for the Maine Alliance for Arts Education, I help teachers learn to incorporate art into the classroom. I have found that once teachers involve themselves in open-ended art experiences, their self-confidence grows, just as it does in young children. They forget that they are "not very creative," or "can't even draw stick people." When teachers realize that they are able to use art materials and develop art projects based around familiar subject matter, creativity takes over, and the ideas begin flowing. The numerous activities described in *Enriching the Curriculum with Art Experiences* will help teachers extend core subjects into reinforcing art experiences.

Acknowledgments

The author is grateful for

- the many people who have helped and encouraged me to write this book;
- my editors and publisher for taking on this project;
- my students who are always eager to participate in art activities;
- my colleagues who allow me the freedom to create;
- the Maine Alliance for the Arts, whose mission is to bring quality arts programs into the schools;
- the many teachers and supervisors who realize the importance of visual creativity;
- my friends who share in the excitement of my work; and
- my family for their love and support.

The author and publishers gratefully acknowledge the following for reviewing the manuscript.

Linda Aulgur
Westminster College
Fulton, MO

Pamela Davis
Henderson State University
Arkadelphia, AR

Elaine Camerin
Daytona Beach Community College
Daytona Beach, FL

Debra Tietze
Rockland Community College
Suffern, NY

About This Book

The activities in this book encourage exploration, self-expression, and creativity, and provide experiences with basic art skills and concepts. Specific concepts and processes are suggested for each creative activity; however, variations in the activities are encouraged to fit individual curricula and needs. It is important that teachers choose subject matter that has meaning to the children. A child's interest, previous art experiences, problem-solving skills, and manipulation skills are all factors that should help in the selection of the art project. For an activity to be appropriate for preschool children, it should be unstructured enough, offer a sensory experience, allow for experimentation and imagination, and provide a sense of success. At the preschool age, manipulation and exploration of art materials are important. The activity is not appropriate if an adult has to do too much of the work.

We need to allow children ample opportunity to become familiar with materials; the simplest of materials can provide deep experiences. Children acquire sensitivity to their surroundings when a helpful adult encourages them to observe, listen, feel, smell, and taste. The adult can ask questions that help children develop an awareness of the elements of art. The basic elements of art (line, shape, color, texture, form, space, and value) are all around us. Activities can be enjoyed that increase awareness in these areas, such as looking for similarities and differences in objects and their surroundings. Simple experiences that increase observation skills, such as looking through colored cellophane papers or using a magnifying glass, also provide children with worthwhile hands-on stimuli.

A teacher or adult is the most important catalyst in providing inspirational stimuli that enriches a child's world. Children can go on nature walks and gather natural materials to be brought into the classroom for observation. This contact with nature can enrich the science curriculum. Hands-on math manipulatives will reinforce analytical thinking and problem solving, which can then be expressed artistically by using geometric shapes and forms. Designing quilts can reinforce learning fractions. Making puppets, books, and story murals can enrich a language arts curriculum. Music can be enjoyed for the qualities of rhythm and tempo and can be expressed in many art experiences using line and color. In social studies, learning about various geographical areas, people, and customs can inspire related art activities. All these curriculum connections and more can be appreciated and explored through art-related experiences.

This book provides a wealth of curriculum-related activities in an easy-to-follow format. Art elements and principles are explained to help the adult reinforce objectives of art activities. Easy-to-use directions for activities are presented along with a list of materials needed for each project. The materials are easily found in most school systems or can be purchased at local stores. The teacher or adult can modify the activities to allow for various media and techniques, subject inspirations, and skill levels.

All activities have the common goal of giving form to an idea and allowing the artists to express their individual feelings about it. The activities afford the opportunity to make personal choices in the creative process. By experimenting with techniques and art media, the artists gain competence in expressing ideas, thoughts, and feelings.

The techniques of drawing, painting, printmaking, cutting and pasting, sculpture, and art appreciation are presented to acquaint the reader with the basic processes. Although briefly described in the section "Techniques in Art," in the Introduction, some of the more advanced processes are not included in the activities in this book, as the skill and comprehension levels are above preschool and elementary school children.

The lessons are arranged in sections by the several subject matters that are explored in most classrooms. Although each lesson is connected to a particular technique, each could also be performed with alternate materials that utilize a different technique. Some multimedia lessons employ more than one material, thus incorporating more than one technique. The subject matter of each activity can also be changed to relate to a specific area of learning for individual classrooms. For example, an activity about birds could also be used with the theme of fish, bugs, flowers, or any subject that is currently being explored in the classroom.

Activity Level Guide

Easy

Medium

Advanced

The lessons in this book were written to be used with preschool children through grade five. The level of the lesson suggests the appropriate skill and developmental level for each activity; however, the activity can be modified to make it more appropriate for other levels. Because children grow and develop at different rates, the lessons in this book are not listed according to chronological age or grade level. They are rated as easy, moderate, or advanced according to developmental stages of the average child. The developmental span in the classroom will vary; some experiences that are labeled easy may seem difficult to some children and some that are labeled advanced could be achieved and enjoyed by younger children.

This is where the art of teaching enters. It is necessary to guide the students in such a way that they will be able to express themselves within the guidelines of the lesson. Remember that the lessons are suggestions and can be modified, simplified, or developed to create the results that promote self-esteem. Although sample pieces are illustrated, assume that creations will vary. Several pieces of art, created by students ranging in age from three to eleven, are included in the color insert. The activity title, along with the child's name and age, is listed below each piece of art. The projects displayed encompass a variety of materials and represent some of the many exciting activities that are described in the text. Viewing children's work makes it possible to imagine the excitement they experience while participating in the activities presented in this book. It is important to allow for individual skills and creative abilities, especially at the preschool level where unstructured experimentation and exploration of materials is most dominant. It is up to the teacher to establish a climate for creative work, provide motivation, and introduce an orderly procedure that allows the children to use their own ideas in developing their work. The teacher should allow the students to work independently until they reach their own stopping points and then try to stimulate their individual thinking and guide them in attaining a new level of achievement.

For each activity, the list of materials provides the basis for a particular lesson, yet alternate materials are also listed for a more open-ended selection. The objectives/concepts list outlines how the lesson allows children to experience art elements, principles, media, and techniques. The activities/process list provides sequential steps to follow, yet leaves room for personal creativity and individual accomplishments.

There are many reasons to create art, including: expressing ideas and feelings, fulfilling a desire to make something, adding aesthetic beauty to the world, learning about and reacting

Why Art Activities Are Important

Art activities strengthen skills in all areas of development: physical, social, emotional, intellectual, and creative.

Art activities increase verbal and nonverbal expression.

Art activities increase motivation and self-discipline.

Art activities contribute to a positive self-image.

Art activities allow expression of personal insights and emotions.

Art activities help to develop concentration.

Art activities help to develop fine motor skills.

Art activities utilize problem-solving techniques.

Art activities contribute to historical and multicultural appreciation.

Art activities help students to create meaning.

Art activities bring things alive.

Art activities connect dreams with reality.

Art activities stimulate communication.

Art activities fill the need for self-expression.

Art activities build a sense of accomplishment.

Art activities interest children.

to the world around us, and for pure enjoyment. It is certainly possible to use the activities listed in this book for the sole purpose of creating artwork. However, to make concrete connections to curriculum it would be beneficial to use visual resources to stimulate, motivate, and reinforce current areas of learning.

Let's imagine that a group of students are learning about flowers in science class. Whether they are preschoolers planting and growing seeds, or older children learning the parts of a plant, an art activity based on flowers would reinforce and visually enhance the children's knowledge of the subject. Besides the learning materials that the teacher has provided for the particular lesson, viewing related visuals can strengthen aesthetic and conceptual knowledge. Art reproductions can be viewed in order to see how other artists have expressed themselves on the same subject. These can be found in local libraries, museums, art supply catalogues, and on calendars or note cards.

To expand upon the science lesson of flowers, actual flowers can be observed along with photographs from books or magazines. Reproductions of the works of Georgia O'Keeffe, Monet, Matisse, and van Gogh, to name only a few artists who created works of flowers, could be viewed and discussed. Having visual connections promotes learning and stimulates students' desire to make their own connections.

Listed with each activity are a few questions to make the discussion meaningful, reinforce the concepts, and connect verbal expression with the visual. This is a time when curriculum learning can be strengthened and enhanced. Sufficient time should be allowed to share and discuss the students' works, as it is important for students to express their ideas and feelings and appreciate the needs and feelings of others. At the end of each lesson activity, curriculum connections are listed citing where the particular art activity can be incorporated into specific areas.

More than one connection to curriculum can be made in many of the listed activities. A lesson on flowers could go beyond its scientific association and incorporate social studies by studying where certain flowers grow, how they are used in societies, and the importance they might bring to cultures. A math activity could involve the number of petals, the geometric shapes of the petals, or the height of the stems. Strengthening the language arts curriculum with art activities can be accomplished by having students relate verbally or in written form to their work. Stories can be shared, poems written, descriptions embellished, or other activities can encourage the use of language in verbal communication. A connection with language arts is always possible through verbal descriptions and discussions. Writing activities could be centered on each lesson by using student imagination and storytelling objectives.

All lessons in this book allow for children to grow creatively, socially, physically, emotionally, and aesthetically. Originality of ideas demonstrates creative growth. Social growth is expressed when a child appreciates the needs and feelings of others. Increasing motor control and eye-hand coordination demonstrates physical growth. Emotional growth will be noted when a child is able to identify with his own work and express personal feelings. The organization of ideas and feeling through the use of materials develops aesthetic growth. Art experiences are rewarding for a child in many instances, therefore it is worthwhile to enhance the curriculum with art experiences. Observation, discovery, exploration, and individual creativity are the important aspects of the art activities. The finished product is a secondary benefit, which enhances the curriculum with related visual works.

Introduction

Art in education should encourage creativity and strengthen visual awareness. As children gain experience in the world of art, they become more sensitive to their environment. Art encourages careful observation and visual literacy. The development of mental imagery facilitates thinking, problem solving, and accomplishing goals.

Children's artwork represents their visual, physical, and emotional experiences. Motor control and eye-hand coordination develop through art activities, as do self-discipline, self-motivation and good work habits. Children learn to take responsibility for themselves and the materials. There are countless opportunities for decision making in an art experience. From the beginning of the creative experience, children make choices about materials, subject matter, and how to utilize the elements of line, shape, color, texture, and so forth.

By externalizing and expressing themselves and their experiences, children gain communication skills, which are an important part of the learning process. The art experience becomes an instrument in discovery. Feelings are created and explored as children experiment with techniques and materials. Sensory awareness is developed through art. When we extend the act of seeing to observing, hearing to listening, and touching to feeling, perception becomes more sensitive and creativity is bolstered.

Creativity involves risk taking; children who feel confident and independent are most open to new creative experiences. Children should be expected to succeed, commended for their efforts, and encouraged to have faith in their own abilities. The creative thinking that the art process requires helps strengthen problem-solving skills. Self-expression and a positive self-concept are formed when children are encouraged to think for themselves and find their own solutions. When artwork is accepted and appreciated for its own qualities there is no pressure to compete, and children gain self-confidence, along with an appreciation of individual differences. These feelings of self-worth enhance all aspects of the children's lives.

Art in Our Schools

There are no boundaries to imagination and inventiveness, and children are excitingly unpredictable in their artistic expression. Without appropriate guidance and encouragement their artistic development can stagnate, leading to feelings of frustration and discouragement.

When children are stimulated and enriched by a teacher's motivation, they are able to more confidently express themselves in a visual way.

Teachers should plan art experiences that help students develop a sense of design and aesthetic form. Students should be challenged to express their reactions and responses in a meaningful way. Discussion of the art elements—design, composition, pattern, line—is necessary if students are to develop their aesthetic awareness. If children only manipulate materials in duplicated patterns and stereotyped decorations, they do not attain the level of expressive, creative, and discriminative personal growth of which each child is capable.

Children create art from what they see, know, and imagine. The presence of a variety of visual stimuli encourages a higher level of both observing and perceiving. When teachers emphasize the use of art elements and art principles, the quality of the children's art increases along with their awareness of their environment.

Most children need some form of motivation, and inspiration may come from many different sources. Teachers act as catalysts in activating motivational experiences. Visual materials, such as illustrations, reproductions, and photographs, should be available for viewing and discussing. Still-life objects should be on hand for exploration and observation. Art materials, as well as techniques, can also be used as motivational tools.

The introduction of the lesson should spark the students' interest and hold their attention. Effective ways to introduce lessons include guided discussions and the viewing of visuals, as well as information about the project theme, such as books or stories, filmstrips, and poems. Teachers should review or explore the major concepts of the lesson while demonstrating the technical process. Simple procedures and techniques should be explained clearly to help children achieve reasonable success. Following the introduction and the distribution of supplies, the creative art activity unfolds when students experiment with materials and explore their understanding of the concepts discussed. This is when the artistic skills of the students are developed. After cleanup, an evaluation or share time reinforces the lesson's objectives and allows students to become aware of each other's thought processes.

For a high-quality art education in the elementary school, it is also necessary to have instruction in art history and art appreciation. Teachers should try to increase the students' visual knowledge of the world. Composition concepts—visual organization and design—should be taught. Students should learn the artistic procedures of drawing, painting, printing, cutting and pasting, and three-dimensional design. In order to ensure strong content, teachers should reinforce concepts from one lesson to another.

The most valuable aspect of creating an art piece is the process, not the finished product. Art activities help students strengthen skills in all areas of development: physical, social, emotional, intellectual, and creative. Children spend a great deal of time in school. Educational growth requires inspiration and stimulation, which the creation and the display of visual art can provide. There are four major areas of stimuli that can be used in art education: direct experience, verbal stimulation, audiovisual aids, and art materials.

Direct experience allows for contact with real objects or events. Field trips outside the school are wonderful but not always possible. Trips within the schoolgrounds can provide a way to view buildings, vehicles, people, trees, fences, and plants. Still-life arrangements provide direct experiences with a wide variety of objects. Physical activity can help children gain knowledge of the human figure, such as jumping, doing exercises, waving, and bending.

Verbal stimulation is often used in conjunction with direct experience. Verbal stimulation is also useful for learning about events and objects that cannot be directly experienced. Objects or places that are far away, in the past or future, and even imaginary can be explored through stories, poems, and conversation.

Audiovisual aids are a wonderful way to engage the students' emotions and build upon concepts. Reproductions, photographs, and other visuals can be displayed, not only for stimulation, but also to make the room more attractive. They are helpful for learning about things that cannot be experienced in the classroom.

Art materials and tools are exciting and can be a source for creative expression. Information must be provided about the use of materials and the steps to be taken in making different art projects.

A teacher should give procedural instruction by demonstrating the same process that the students will be expected to follow. It is easier for students to understand and remember procedural instruction if they can see a demonstration as well as hear verbal instruction. Finished examples help students envision the project they are about to make; however, avoid making pictures that children do not have the skill to duplicate. They can acquire ideas from the samples but should be discouraged from trying to copy the models. Teachers should show students that they are interested in their ideas and their work. Encourage children to do their own artwork by responding in a positive way to their efforts.

Students need some instruction in composition. Visual organization encompasses balance, unity, and variety. Balance is achieved by making one side equal to the other in visual weight and the ability to attract attention. Unity is achieved by manipulating the elements of visual form, which include line, color, shape, and texture. Variety can be demonstrated by using different colors, shapes, textures, and patterns. It is desirable to maintain a balance between unity and variety.

It is important to exhibit children's art because it creates a supportive environment. It pleases children to see their work and helps build self-confidence. There is also educational value to displays of the students' artwork. By viewing how other students have handled a given topic, students gain appreciation for styles and techniques that are different from their own.

To build an art curriculum, consider the following six categories.

1. Decide on objectives in the areas of knowledge, attitude, and skill.
2. Select the content. Strive to build children's understanding of themselves and the world around them, of composition and artistic procedures, and of art history and appreciation.
3. Choose an activity. Activities should include a variety of techniques, such as drawing, painting, printing, cutting and pasting, and three-dimensional design.
4. Select teaching techniques. These include demonstrations, discussions, and visual aids.
5. Organize the lessons into a learning sequence by considering the connections between them.
6. Evaluate the lesson. Achievement cannot be measured only by the products. Art education is concerned with children's overall development, therefore we must measure verbal as well as visual knowledge and skill, as well as attitudes.

Classroom management seems to require more effort during art classes due to the movement of the students and supplies. Under teacher direction, much of the work can be done by the students, who distribute and collect supplies, clean tools, pick up the room, and display the art. Although it is sometimes easier for the teacher to do a considerable amount, students should be involved for many reasons. It builds positive work habits, helps develop responsibility, gives a sense of belonging, promotes cooperative behavior, and provides satisfaction. Once a routine is developed with systematic methods, the procedures should flow smoothly.

Primarily artists create art for one or more of the following three reasons.

1. To recreate the physical world as they see it.
2. To explore an idea or feeling.
3. To create an interesting design.

There are many ways to nurture creativity.

1. Teach the children to observe the world around them. Describe scenes or pictures. Play adjective games to enhance awareness of detail (e.g., fuzzy, fluffy slippers). Compare and contrast by pointing out similarities and differences.
2. Expose the children to art. Visit galleries and museums. Look at books and reproductions. Calendars are a wonderful source for reproductions of master artists.
3. Provide materials and a workspace.
4. Talk about art.

> Describe the art elements: line, shape, color, texture, and so on.
> Analyze the composition: repetition, variation, balance, and so on. How are the elements put together?
> Interpret the meaning. What do you think the artist is trying to tell us?
> Evaluate the work. Did the artist accomplish what you feel he or she was trying to do? Do you like the work? Why or why not?

There are many different ideas that can be used as the basis for an art lesson. Design work is a playful, relaxed, adventurous way to visualize. Exploration with line, shape, color, and pattern can be accomplished with a variety of materials. Projects about the self, such as self-portraits, name designs, home, and family help children gain self-understanding and confidence. Art helps children understand their feelings, such as likes, dislikes, fears, and other emotions. When children become more observant of details they are better able to express themselves.

Design

The discovery of design is the beginning of an ongoing adventure. Understanding and organizing the elements and principles of design is what guides the creative work into a meaningful experience. Even very young children can gain an awareness and appreciation of the different elements. The opportunity for a child to feel objects of different textures (e.g., sandpaper, cotton, bark) gives a concrete meaning to the element of texture. Art has a language that describes the basic parts and the guidelines for putting the parts together. Artists arrange these parts or elements to express their ideas. Introducing the art language to young children, and then reinforcing and emphasizing it with each art experience deepens their visual creativity. Preschool children become familiar with the art elements when they describe the shape, color, and texture of objects.

Artists design or arrange their artwork by combining the different art elements into an organized whole according to the principles of art. The seven elements of design—line, shape, form, texture, space, color, and value—describe the artist's visual tools. The principles of design—balance, emphasis, variety, unity, movement, rhythm, and repetition—describe how the artist puts the elements together to create a piece of artwork. A unified design is one in which all the parts work together. Artists decide, instinctively or deliberately, how they will use the elements in their work. By placing or combining elements in certain areas, the artist can balance the work. By using combinations of sizes, colors, or values, an artist can add variety to a composition. Style refers to the particular way artists use the art elements, principles, techniques, and materials to achieve unity and express themselves.

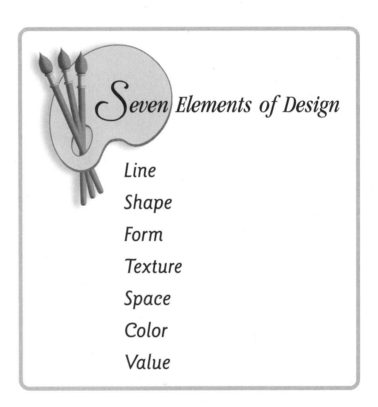

Seven Elements of Design

Line

Shape

Form

Texture

Space

Color

Value

Elements of Design

Line

A line can be described as an elongated continuous mark made by a moving point. Drawing the edges of objects in outline form is the most common form of line made by children. A line that shows the edges of an object is called a contour line. Different types of lines can create different effects, movements, directions, or textures. Many artists use outlines to add interest or unity to their work. By emphasizing a line, clarity, interest, and accent are added. Some artists, however, try to eliminate the outline and create a shimmering effect.

Elements of Line Design

Sometimes when you can't think of what to draw, it helps to think of the elements of line design.

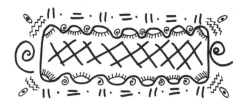

These can be put together many ways using any kind of art material. Repeating some parts can create interesting patterns and textures.

Lines that suggest movement can influence feelings. Strength and stability can be suggested by vertical lines that go up and down. Side-to-side horizontal lines portray calmness. Diagonal lines express tension, and curved lines imply flowing movement.

Shape

Shape is an area that is made by one or more of the other elements. Because they have only the two dimensions of height and width, shapes are flat. A shape can be created by joining a continuous line with itself or by joining several lines. Color or texture can also create a shape.

Form

Form is a three-dimensional object. It has depth as well as height and width. Mass and volume are two features of form. The mass is the outside size and the volume is the inside space. Cubes, spheres, cylinders, and pyramids are examples of forms.

Texture

Texture implies surface quality, the way things feel or look like they would feel. Some artwork can literally have a textural quality that can be felt. Other work can feel smooth to the touch but appear to be rough or bumpy.

Space

Space is the area above, below, between, around, or within things. Actual space can be found in three-dimensional art forms where one can view the work from different viewpoints and see different shapes and images. Three-dimensional space has height, width, and depth, whereas two-dimensional space has only height and width. Artists can create the illusion of depth on flat surfaces by incorporating several techniques, such as overlapping shapes, making distant shapes smaller or higher in the picture, using less detail and less intense colors in distant shapes, or using diagonal lines so that objects appear to be extending back into space.

Color

Color has three qualities: hue, intensity, and value. Hue is the actual name of the color, such as blue or red. The intensity refers to the quality of brightness and purity of the color. The stronger, purer, or brighter the color, the more intense it is. The value of a color refers to the lightness or darkness of the hue. An artist can change the value of a hue by adding black or white to it. By adding black, a hue becomes darker and is considered a shade. Adding white to a hue lightens it, and creates a tint.

A color wheel can assist in understanding color (see color insert). The color wheel is usually divided into twelve sections, with the three primary colors spaced equally around the wheel. Red, yellow, and blue are called the primary colors because they can be mixed with each other to make different colors, but they cannot be created by mixing other colors.

Orange, green, and purple are called secondary colors because it takes two primary colors to make them. On the color wheel, secondary colors are found midway between the primary colors. Red mixed with yellow makes orange, blue mixed with yellow makes green, and blue mixed with red makes purple.

Intermediate or tertiary colors are located between the primary and the secondary colors. They can be made by mixing different amounts of two primary colors. For example, adding more red to a mixture of red and yellow will produce an intermediate color of red orange. Adding more yellow than red will produce the intermediate color of yellow-orange.

The colors that are next to each other on the color wheel are called analogous colors and are closely related. Red, red-orange, and orange would be considered analogous colors. Complementary colors are opposite each other on the color wheel. When two complementary colors are added together in equal amounts they produce a neutral tone. If a small amount of a hue's complement is added to it, the hue's intensity decreases.

Colors that appear on the blue, green, and purple side of the color wheel are considered cool colors, as they suggest an association with water or sky. Cool colors appear to recede into the background of a picture. The colors on the red, yellow, and orange side of the color wheel are considered warm colors. They suggest the warmth of the sun and fire. Warm colors seem to advance toward the viewer.

Value

Value is an important element even if there is no color in the artwork, such as in black-and-white drawings, prints, and photographs. A gradual change in value can produce concave or convex surfaces and lend itself to the appearance of three dimensions.

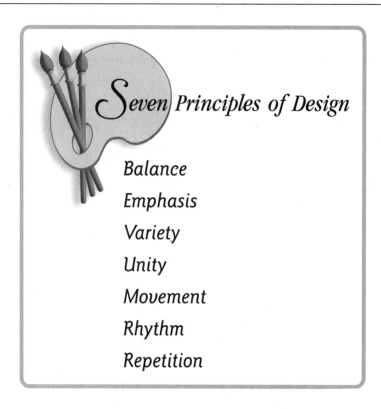

Seven Principles of Design

Balance

Emphasis

Variety

Unity

Movement

Rhythm

Repetition

Principles of Design

Balance

Artists create balance by using the elements of design to create a feeling of stability and equilibrium. Balance can be symmetrical, asymmetrical, or radial. Symmetrical balance is the simplest type of balance—the two sides of the work are exactly the same. Asymmetrical balance is more informal, and takes into account that qualities such as size, shape, and color affect the relative visual weight of the objects. Radial balance is centered around a point.

Emphasis

Emphasis refers to the part of an artwork that attracts the viewer's attention. To avoid monotonous or uninteresting works, an artist will often add contrast in order to bring attention to a certain area, thus creating a center of interest.

Variety

Variety is a way to increase visual interest through diversity or change. The use of variety can create intricate and complicated relationships. It is important, however, that the work does not seem too confusing, and there is a sense of harmony or unity involved.

Unity

Unity or harmony is created when similar elements are used in order to tie the parts of the work together into a whole. Both variety and unity are important in a work of art; unity creates a feeling of oneness and togetherness, and variety attracts attention and holds the interest of the viewer.

Movement

Movement is the principle that describes a sensation of action in an artwork. It guides the eye of the viewer throughout the artwork, by placing the elements so that the eye follows a certain path.

Rhythm

Rhythm is closely related to movement. Repeated elements are placed so that they create a visual beat or tempo. The viewer's eye bounces quickly or glides smoothly from one element to the next.

Repetition

Repetition or pattern describes when an element is used over and over again. The combination of elements must be repeated three or more times in order to create a pattern.

Techniques in Art

Drawing

Drawing is the act of making lines on a surface. Anything that produces a mark can be used for drawing, but the most common tools are pencils, crayons (oil and wax), chalk, pastels, charcoal, markers, and pen and ink. In early times pencil drawings were more widely used for sketching or for small studies, because the thin lines of pencil tend to lose impact when surrounded by a lot of space. Later on, drawings came to be considered a major art form. Artists who specialize in pencil drawings usually work on a small scale. The type of carbon or graphite in pencils ranges from hard to soft and can produce lines and values from gray to black. Colored pencils add the dimension of color to pencil drawing. It is important to provide opportunities for drawing that allow the making of details. Techniques can be explored that discover the potential of line, such as thickness, direction, length, and type. Drawing is the most fundamental art process and the most widely practiced, starting with the very young child making crayon marks on paper and progressing to an adult doodling on a pad of paper at a business meeting. The style of a drawing is determined by the artist's purpose and chosen medium.

Painting

Artists may select portraits, landscapes, still lifes, everyday objects, events, or decorative works as the subjects of their paintings. The time and place in which an artist is living also influences the subject depicted in a painting. Different results can be achieved by different kinds of paints. Oil, tempera, encaustic, watercolor, and acrylic paints all have three basic ingredients. Pigment is what gives the paint its color. It is a fine powder that can be produced chemically or by grinding up a part of earth, stone, or mineral. The liquid that holds the pigment together is called the binder. Tempera paint uses egg whites, oil paint uses linseed oil, encaustic uses melted wax, watercolor uses a mixture of water and gum arabic, and acrylic paint uses an acrylic polymer. A material called a solvent is used to thin the binder.

Paintbrushes come in many sizes and shapes. They can be flat, pointed, long, short, stiff or flexible. Artists sometimes apply paint with objects other than brushes to achieve different effects. To make rough, heavy, textural strokes, a palette knife can be used to apply the paint directly to the canvas.

Printmaking

Printmaking allows the artist to transfer a design from one surface to another and to create multiple images. There are a variety of printmaking processes, ranging from the very simple (applying ink to a thumb and pressing to make a thumbprint) to the very complicated, with multiple color designs. There are four basic methods of printmaking: relief, intaglio, lithography, and screen printing.

When the image to be printed is raised above the surface of the printing tool, the method is called relief printing. Areas are cut or smoothed away from the sections that will be printed. The raised surfaces are covered with ink and pressed against paper to create the image.

Intaglio printing includes etching and engraving, and is a process where ink fills in lines that have been cut away. After the smooth surface is clean of ink the printing plate is pressed, causing the inked lines to transfer onto the paper.

Lithography is a process where an image is drawn with a special greasy crayon directly on a block of limestone, zinc, or aluminum. It is then treated chemically and the surface is watered down and then inked. The ink sticks to the crayoned area and is transferred to paper after going through a press.

In screen printing, a stencil is placed on a fabric screen that has been stretched and ink is pushed through the screen onto the paper with a squeegee.

Sculpture

Sculpture includes three-dimensional forms in various sizes, shapes, and materials. They may represent actual objects or expressions of emotions. Relief sculptures are forms that extend out from a flat surface but are still attached to the surface. High-relief sculptures project into space greatly, whereas bas-relief forms only slightly protrude from the background.

Sculptures in the round can be viewed from all sides, even though they might be meant to be viewed from certain positions. Choice of materials is important in sculpture. Some common materials include clay, stone, metal, and wood. Sculptures can be created by modeling, carving, assembling, or casting. Modeling refers to the shaping of pliable material such as clay, wax, or plaster around some type of armature or support system. Carving is the chipping or cutting away of a material, usually stone or wood.

Casting involves pouring a liquid substance into a mold, which then hardens. Wax, clay, and plaster are a few casting materials. During the assembly process, materials are joined together to create the three-dimensional structure.

A sculptural form that moves in space is called kinetic art. It can be moved by air, water, or motor. Mobiles are one type of kinetic art.

Cutting and Pasting

The two-dimensional process of cutting and pasting is one in which a variety of materials can be used. Paper is easily acquired and can be found in many different colors, thicknesses, and textures. A collage can be composed of paper, cloth, string, magazine pictures, or photographs. Glue sticks, white glue, and rubber cement can be utilized as adhesives. Mixed-media pictures sometimes incorporate paints with the other materials.

Art Appreciation

Looking at and discussing artwork is an important part of the art experience. Sharing personal feelings, likes and dislikes, about an artwork is often as far as conversations progress unless further exploration is encouraged. There are two ways to understand and appreciate artwork, the art history approach and the art criticism approach. Both approaches make use of four steps. They are description, analysis, interpretation, and judgment.

In the art history approach, description refers to who painted the picture, when it was painted, and where. The art criticism approach to description involves describing what is in the artwork, identifying the details, and describing the elements. The art history approach to analysis examines the style of the work, which is the way the elements and principles are used to express ideas and feelings. Sometimes more than one artist paints with similar features and techniques. The art criticism approach to analysis involves concentrating on how the work is organized. The principles of art are important in determining the qualities of design. Art history interpretation considers how artists are influenced by the world around them. Art criticism interpretation centers around the feelings, ideas, and meanings that are communicated to the viewer. Art historians judge the importance of a work of art according to its place in the history of art. The art critic's judgment relies on the aesthetic qualities of a work of art and if it succeeds according to the theories he or she favors.

Helpful Hints to Avoid Messy and Time-Wasting Art Experiences

Organization is the key to a positive art experience in the classroom. Simple procedures and techniques need to be clearly explained. A step-by-step presentation and completed samples for the children to view will help them visualize possible approaches to the activity. The creative process should begin immediately after the presentation, before the children lose the enthusiasm sparked in discussion. Prior preparation of materials will ensure a smooth transition into creative work time. Having students' work areas arranged in groups is helpful for sharing of materials. If it is necessary to cover the work space because of the materials being used, newspapers that have been previously stacked, one double page at a time, will facilitate the setup. Old shower curtains or plastic tablecloths hung over tables or group desks also work well to keep surfaces clean. In classrooms that do not have sinks available, teachers can set up two three-gallon plastic tubs. One should have clean water and the other will be used to dump the dirty water in.

Egg cartons are wonderful containers for paint. They keep the colors carefully separated in small quantities and can be thrown away at the end of the activity. Plastic containers are helpful for organizing and distributing markers, crayons, and chalk, to group work areas.

After an art activity it is important for students to be involved in a cooperative cleanup. This should take place after work time and before share time. The first children to finish their projects can begin gathering up materials, collecting art tools, and throwing away unusable materials. This should be done in a quiet, orderly manner so as not to disturb the students who are finishing their work.

It is necessary to instill a cooperative atmosphere where everyone helps in the cleanup when they finish their work. In order for children to fully appreciate art materials, they must be responsible for taking proper care of them. If a positive attitude is developed early on, then it is possible for the children to work in a creative atmosphere from beginning to end.

Activities

Scissors Design

Objectives/Concepts

1. To work with shape and color.
2. To work with positive and negative shapes and spaces.
3. To work with repetition.
4. To experiment with design elements and principles.
5. To experiment with drawing technique.

Technique

Drawing

Materials

12 in. x 18 in. white paper
Black marker
Crayons (wax or oil)
Pencil

Alternate Materials

Colored markers, colored pencils

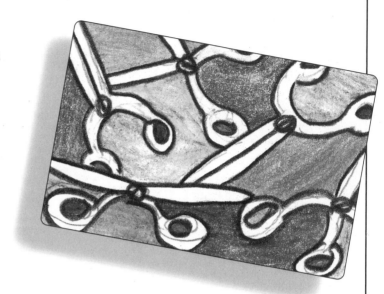

Activities/Process

1. Discuss positive and negative shapes and spaces.
2. Trace scissors with pencil all around the 12 in. x 18 in. paper so that a part of each scissors is touching another scissors or the edge of the paper. Scissors can be opened or closed to create different positions.
3. Go over the pencil lines with black marker.
4. Color in the negative spaces with crayon.

Questions for Discussion

What is a negative shape? What types of colors did you choose for your design? Are any of the scissors positioned similarly? What types of shapes did the scissors form in the negative areas? How many times did you trace the scissors? Can you find similar shapes?

Share Time/Evaluation

_____
_____
_____
_____

Curriculum Connection

Math

Circles and Lines

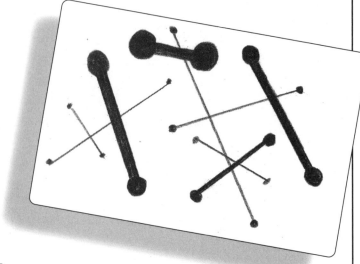

Objectives/Concepts

1. To work with a variety of line lengths and thicknesses.
2. To work with a variety of circle sizes.
3. To overlap.
4. To intersect.
5. To experiment with drawing technique.
6. To experiment with cutting and pasting.

Technique

Drawing, Cutting and Pasting

Materials

12 in. x 18 in. white paper
Black marker
Black construction paper circles in different sizes
Black construction paper lines in different lengths and thicknesses
Scissors
Glue

Alternate Materials

Colored markers, colored circles, colored lines, crayons, yarn

Activities/Process

1. Discuss varieties of a straight line (thick, thin, long, short).
2. Discuss different sizes of circles.
3. Discuss design elements and how to fill the page with a variety of straight lines and circles.
4. With a marker draw small dots and lines on the white paper.
5. Glue black paper circles and lines of different sizes on top of the drawn dots and lines so that some intersect and overlap.

Questions for Discussion

What is similar about the lines in your picture? What is different about the lines in your picture? How are the circles different? Do you have any circles that are the same? How many? Do some circles and lines seem closer to you than others? Which ones and why? What shapes were made from the overlapped and intersected lines?

Share Time/Evaluation

_____
_____
_____
_____

Curriculum Connection

Math

Looking out the Window, by Bud, Age 8

Grapevines, by Cassandra, Age 3

Giraffe, by Jordan, Age 5

Tall Birds, by Elizabeth, Age 6

Positive and Negative Leaves Design, by Caroline, Age 7

Looking in the Grass with a Magnifying Glass, by Taylor, Age 8

Winter Tree, by Deidre, Age 7

Depths of the Ocean, by Bradley, Age 11

Textured Quilt,
by Sarah, Age 6

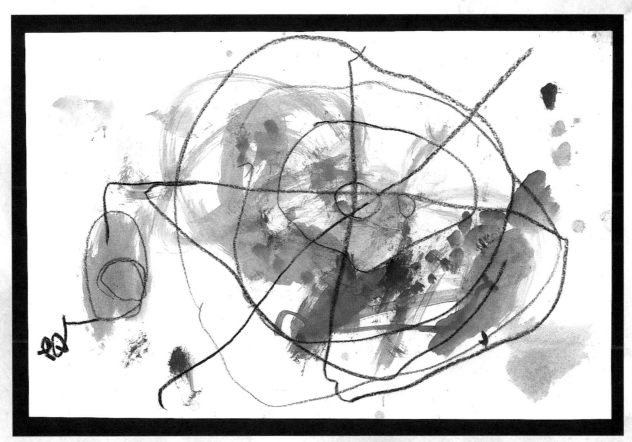

Spider and Web, by Matthew, Age 3

Sock Puppets, by Addie, Age 6

Colorful Bird, by Connor, Age 7

Painted Buildings, by Raechel, Age 5

Dots and Dashes, by Kate, Age 6

Faces in the Crowd, by Colin, Age 5

Mountain Range, by Curtis, Age 6

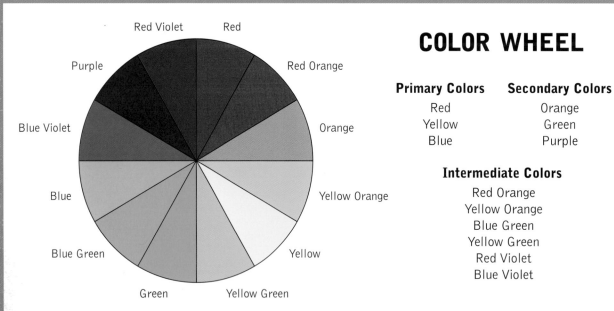

COLOR WHEEL

Red Violet
Red
Purple
Red Orange
Blue Violet
Orange
Blue
Yellow Orange
Blue Green
Yellow
Green
Yellow Green

Primary Colors
Red
Yellow
Blue

Secondary Colors
Orange
Green
Purple

Intermediate Colors
Red Orange
Yellow Orange
Blue Green
Yellow Green
Red Violet
Blue Violet

Straight Line Design

Objectives/Concepts

1. To work with straight lines.
2. To use horizontal, vertical, and diagonal lines.
3. To find shapes within intersecting lines.
4. To work with pattern.
5. To experiment with drawing technique.

Technique

Drawing

Materials

9 in. x 12 in. white drawing paper
Pencil
One colored pencil
Ruler

Alternate Materials

Colored markers, crayons (wax or oil), Styrofoam printing plate, printing ink, printing plate, brayer

Activities/Process

1. Discuss variations of a straight line (horizontal, vertical, diagonal).
2. Make five little marks along one edge of the paper, spacing them so they cover the entire side.
3. Repeat step 2 on the remaining three sides.
4. With a ruler draw a straight line attaching one mark to another mark on any of the other three sides.
5. Continue drawing lines from one mark to another using each mark only once until all the marks have been used.
6. With the colored pencil, fill in some of the shapes formed from the intersecting lines with solid color.
7. Fill in some of the shapes formed with straight horizontal lines, straight vertical lines, and straight diagonal lines.

Questions for Discussion

What happened when lines intersected each other? Can you name some of the shapes formed? What direction are your lines going in? What is similar about the lines? What is different about the lines? Did you notice any difference if your lines were close together or further apart?

Share Time/Evaluation

_____
_____
_____
_____

Curriculum Connection

Math

Red Magic Ball

Objectives/Concepts

1. To work with line, shape, and color.
2. To use imagination.
3. To experiment with drawing technique.
4. To create emphasis.

Technique

Drawing

Materials

12 in. x 18 in. white paper
2 in. red construction paper circle
Black marker
Crayons (wax or oil)
Glue

Alternate Materials

Colored markers, watercolor paints, tempera paints, chalk, pastels, assorted colored papers

Activities/Process

1. Pretend the red circle is a magic ball and when it bounces it becomes part of something that has a circle. Give a few suggestions such as a traffic light, the inside of a flower, the face of a watch, the inside of a mouse ear, etc. To make things exciting for the class a small red ball can be gently tossed from one student to the next. Each time a child has the ball she needs to think of an object that has a circle as part of it (the color does not matter).
2. Glue a red circle to the white paper.
3. With black marker make the circle into something.
4. Draw a scene around the object.
5. Color in with crayons to complete the picture.

Questions for Discussion

How did you use your circle? Did you use any patterns or textures in your picture? Did you have to make the object larger or smaller than normal to have the red circle be part of it? Where is your object?

Share Time/Evaluation

_____
_____
_____
_____

Curriculum Connection

Language Arts

Styrofoam Block Printing

Objectives/Concepts

1. To work with line and shape.
2. To prepare a printing block in the subtractive (etching) method.
3. To create a mirror (reverse) image.
4. To create texture.
5. To experiment with printing technique.

Technique

Drawing, Printing

Materials

Styrofoam sheet	Pencil
Colored paper at least 1 inch larger than the Styrofoam on all sides	Printing ink
	Inking plate
	Brayer or roller

Alternate Materials

Styrofoam grocery tray, pen, nail, or other sharp object

Activities/Process

1. Discuss geometric shapes, lines, and sizes. Instead of a geometric design, the subject for the print could be based on the theme being reinforced in the curriculum, such as animals in the jungle, birds in the forest, or fish in the ocean.
2. With pencil draw a picture directly on the Styrofoam. Sketches can be made on scrap paper first; it is important to stress that once a line is drawn on the Styrofoam it can not be erased. Explain that whatever is being drawn on the Styrofoam will appear reversed in the print.
3. Make lines strong enough to push below the surface of the Styrofoam.
4. At a designated printing area that has been set up, roll the ink smoothly over the Styrofoam.
5. Back at individual workspaces place paper on top of the inked Styrofoam and rub gently with the palm of the hand.
6. Lift the paper to expose the print.
7. The same piece of Styrofoam can be used repeatedly to make more prints by rolling over it each time with ink before printing. If any lines are not showing they might need to be traced over again with the pencil to make them a little deeper.

Questions for Discussion

What is printing? How did you prepare your Styrofoam for printing? What is a mirror image? Where did you create texture? What happened if you rolled too much ink on the Styrofoam? What made it have too much ink? Is there a difference between your prints?

Share Time/Evaluation

_____
_____
_____

Curriculum Connection

Science, Math

Apple Design

Objectives/Concepts

1. To work with shape, line, and color.
2. To work with overlapping.
3. To work with repetition.
4. To create rhythm.
5. To experiment with drawing technique.

Technique

Drawing

Materials

12 in. x 18 in. white paper
4½ in. x 6 in. oak tag
Pencil
Scissors
Oil crayons

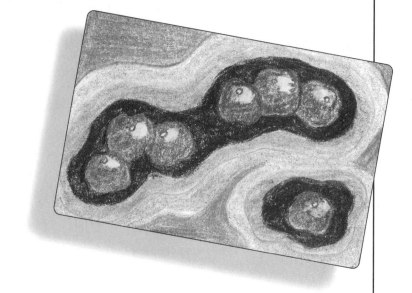

Alternate Materials

Colored chalk, tempera paints, watercolor paints

Activities/Process

1. Discuss and view visuals of apples.
2. Draw a large apple on the oak tag.
3. Cut out the apple and trace it on the paper. Try to create a rhythm by overlapping a few times, leaving spaces, and working the line of apples around the paper.
4. Color in the apples.
5. Draw a line around the apples making a thin shape enclosing them. Color the shape. This can be done in groups.
6. Using another color draw another line around the first creating another shape. Color in.
7. Continue until all the space is filled in. Limit the color choice to no more than three colors.

Questions for Discussion

Where did you overlap? How did the position of the apples allow for the rhythm of the design? Why did you choose the colors that you did? Does your eye flow smoothly from one area to another?

Share Time/Evaluation

Curriculum Connection

Science, Math

Cut-Paper Still Life

Objectives/Concepts

1. To work with line, shape, and color.
2. To work with still-life composition.
3. To work with overlapping.
4. To create texture.
5. To create a three-dimensional quality.
6. To experiment with color blending.
7. To work with proportion.
8. To experiment with cutting and pasting technique.

Technique

Drawing, Cutting and Pasting

Materials

12 in. x 18 in. dark blue or black paper
Assorted colored construction paper
Colored chalk
Scissors

Glue
Still-life objects (fruit, vegetables,
   a piece of fabric, vase with flowers,
   or a plant)

Alternate Materials

Variety of papers, magazine photos of fruits, vegetables, and plants, pastels, crayons (wax or oil)

Activities/Process

1. Discuss and view visuals of still lifes including fruits, vegetables, plants, and fabric.
2. Set up a classroom still life to view.
3. Cut geometric shapes and forms to represent the objects in the still life.
4. Cut a form representing a piece of material to drape under and around the fruit.
5. With colored chalk blend the colors of the objects and add highlights and shadows to create a three-dimensional effect.
6. Add lines and shape with colored chalk to represent folds of the fabric.
7. Glue the paper fabric to the paper.
8. Arrange and glue down the still-life objects making sure to overlap.

Questions for Discussion

What is a still life? How did we create a feeling of three dimensions with the paper fruit? Where did you overlap? What is a highlight? What did you do to make the paper seem like a folded piece of fabric? How did you blend some of your colors? What is composition? What is proportion?

Share Time/Evaluation

Curriculum Connection

Science, Social Studies, Math

Fruit Still Life

Objectives/Concepts

1. To work with line and shape.
2. To experiment with color mixing.
3. To work with overlapping.
4. To work with proportion.

Technique

Painting

Materials

12 in. x 18 in. white paper
Black crayon
Watercolor paints
Still-life objects

Alternate Materials

Tempera paint, crayons (wax or oil), colored chalk

Activities/Process

1. Discuss and view visuals of fruit and still lifes.
2. Set up a class room still life for viewing.
3. With black crayon draw a still-life arrangement of fruit, making sure some fruits overlap each other. Draw large enough to fill the paper.
4. Paint in with watercolor paints.
5. The space around the still life can also be painted.

Questions for Discussion

What is a still life? How do artists arrange the objects in their still lifes? What are some of the shapes of your fruit? How do the sizes compare with each other? Which fruit is overlapping another fruit? How did you mix some of your colors? Are any of your fruit the same?

Share Time/Evaluation

_____
_____
_____
_____

Curriculum Connection

Science, Social Studies, Math

Grapevines

Objectives/Concepts

1. To work with line, shape, and color.
2. To experiment with the printmaking technique.
3. To create texture.

Technique

Drawing, Printing

Materials

12 in. x 18 in. white paper
Crayons (wax or oil)
Purple paint

Alternate Materials

Chalk, pastel construction paper, sticky dots

Activities/Process

1. Discuss and show visuals of grapevines.
2. Using a black crayon draw a curly line around the paper.
3. Thicken the line on both sides with brown crayon.
4. Add green leaves.
5. Add little brown or black curly lines.
6. Using fingertips and purple paint, print bunches of grapes hanging from the vine.

Questions for Discussion

How do grapes grow? Are all grapes the same color and size? How did you make different-sized grapes on your paper? Can you tell me something about printing? Why do the colors of some of your grapes look different?

Share Time/Evaluation

_____

_____

_____

_____

Curriculum Connection

Science, Social Studies, Math

Chalk Dipped in Paint Still Life

Objectives/Concepts

1. To work with color, shape, and texture.
2. To use proportion.
3. To use overlapping.
4. To create a three-dimensional quality.
5. To work with highlights.
6. To compose a still-life arrangement.

Technique

Drawing

Materials

12 in. x 18 in. dark blue paper
Colored chalk
White tempera paint
Objects for still life (fruits, vegetables, plants, etc.)

Alternative Materials

Pastels, charcoal, colored tempera paints

Activities/Process

1. Discuss still lifes and their arrangements. View reproductions of still-life paintings. Set up a classroom still life. If nutrition or health is in the curriculum, it can be reinforced at this time.
2. Talk about the size, shape, color, and texture of the fruits and vegetables and point out the highlights.
3. Demonstrate dipping chalk into the white paint and drawing. This will create texture and highlights.

Questions for Discussion

What is a still life? How do artists arrange still lifes? What did you do to make your fruit look three-dimensional?

Share Time/Evaluation

_____
_____
_____
_____

Curriculum Connection

Science, Social Studies, Math

Vegetable Print

Objectives/Concepts

1. To work with line, shape, and color.
2. To create texture.
3. To use repetition.
4. To experiment with printing technique.

Technique

Printing

Materials

9 in. x 12 in. white paper cut in the shape of a canning jar
9 in. x 12 in. gray paper glued under the white, cut to leave a
   ½ in. border
Variety of vegetables
Tempera paints
2 in. x 3 in. white paper
Black fine-line marker

Alternate Materials

Material, ribbon, stamp pad

Activities/Process

1. Discuss and view visuals of vegetables and canning.
2. Paint the end cross-section of a vegetable. (First make sure the vegetable is dry.)
3. Press the vegetable on the white paper. Lift and press again.
4. Repeat painting and pressing the vegetable until the jar-shaped paper is filled in.
5. Write the vegetable name on the white paper. The date can also be added.
6. If desired, material can be cut and glued to the lid or a ribbon can be tied to the top.

Questions for Discussion

Name some vegetables. Does anyone have a family garden? Does your family prepare vegetables to save for a later time? What do they do to keep the vegetables safe for eating? What is printing? What happened if the vegetable was wet? What happened if there was too much paint on the vegetable? What if there wasn't enough paint?

Share Time/Evaluation

_____
_____
_____
_____

Curriculum Connection

Science, Social Studies, Math

Food Face

Objectives/Concepts

1. To work with line, shape, and color.
2. To work with texture.
3. To work with facial features.
4. To work with proportion.
5. To experiment with cutting and pasting technique.

Technique

Cutting and Pasting

Materials

12 in. x 18 in. black paper
9 in. x 12 in. colored paper (choice of salmon, tan, or brown)
4½ in. x 6 in. colored paper (choice of salmon, tan, or brown)
Magazine with food photographs
Scissors

Alternate Materials

Dried food such as beans, popcorn, nuts, cereal

Activities/Process

1. Discuss and show visuals on food and nutrition.
2. Discuss and show visuals on heads, facial features, and hair.
3. Round the corners of the 9 x 12 colored paper to make an oval.
4. Glue it to the middle of the 12 x 18 paper in a vertical position.
5. Glue the 4½ x 6 colored paper below the oval head for the neck.
6. Look through the magazine for various foods that can be used for the facial features and the hair. A bowl of spaghetti might be cut out and glued down for the hair. It will be necessary to find two of the same foods for the eyes and ears.

Questions for Discussion

Why is it important to eat healthy foods? When eating foods do you think the way they look makes a difference? How are the textures of foods different? What texture is the food you used for the hair in your picture? Was it hard to find two of the same foods in the same magazine? Did you find similar advertisements in different magazines? How are foods similar or different in other countries?

Share Time/Evaluation

_____
_____
_____
_____

Curriculum Connection

Science, Social Studies

City Street

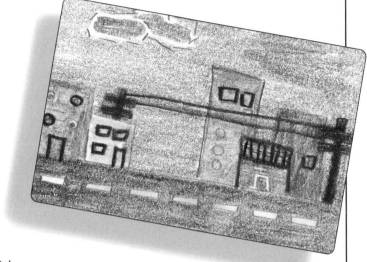

Objectives/Concepts

1. To work with color, line, and shape.
2. To work with overlapping.
3. To experience printing techniques.

Technique

Cutting and Pasting, Printing

Materials

12 in. x 18 in. blue paper

Assorted construction paper squares and
   rectangles

2 in. x 12 in. black paper

Tempera paint (black and white)

Glue

Printing materials (sponges, marker caps, craft sticks,
   Q-tips, small strips of corrugated cardboard, etc.)

Alternate Materials

Colored chalk, pastels, crayons (wax or oil), assorted papers, markers

Activities/Process

1. Discuss and view visuals of buildings and city environments.
2. Glue black paper on bottom of blue paper to represent a street.
3. Arrange and glue squares and rectangles to make a row of buildings on top of the street.
4. With white paint, print short lines on the black street.
5. With printing materials, print windows, doors, streetlights, telephone wires, etc.

Questions for Discussion

What does a city street look like? What buildings are in front of other buildings? What is printing? How did
you make some of the details in your picture? What printing materials did you use and what kind of shapes
did they make?

Share Time/Evaluation

Curriculum Connection

Social Studies

E

Painted Buildings

Objectives/Concepts

1. To work with a variety of rectangles and squares.
2. To use primary colors.
3. To mix secondary colors.

Technique

Painting

Materials

12 in. x 18 in. white or manila paper
Tempera paints (red, yellow, blue, and black)

Alternate Materials

Watercolor paints, oil crayons, construction paper

Activities/Process

1. Discuss painting technique.
2. Discuss primary colors and how to make secondary colors.
3. Discuss and view visuals of buildings in a city neighborhood.
4. Using primary and secondary colors, paint a variety of squares and rectangles for buildings.
5. Outline buildings with black paint.
6. Add black windows and doors.
7. Paint sky.

Questions for Discussion

Have you ever been to a neighborhood in a city where the buildings are lined up right next to each other? Why do you think it is that way? Where would you be standing to see the buildings in a line like these? How many windows are in each building? Which building has more windows? What are the primary colors? What happened when you mixed two colors together?

Share Time/Evaluation

_____
_____
_____
_____

Curriculum Connection

Social Studies, Language Arts, Math

Bus Field Trip

Objectives/Concepts

1. To work with line, shape, and color.
2. To work with overlapping.
3. To create distance.
4. To create texture.
5. To experiment with drawing technique.

Technique

Drawing

Materials

12 in. x 18 in. white paper
3 in. x 12 in. black paper
Precut stencil of a yellow bus
Crayons (wax or oil)
Glue

Alternate Materials

Colored construction paper, watercolor paints, colored markers

Activities/Process

1. Discuss a recent or upcoming field trip.
2. Glue the black paper to the bottom of the white paper.
3. Add details to the yellow paper bus or draw and cut out your own bus.
4. Glue the bus to the black road.
5. With crayons, draw the scenery around the bus as if you were going on a class field trip. For example, a trip to the apple orchard might have several apple trees, baskets or bags of apples near the trees, ladders leaning on the trees or children reaching and climbing to pick apples. There might be a place where apples are sold or a machine to make cider.

Questions for Discussion

Discuss the class field trip, what the students will see, or what they have already experienced. Have them talk about their pictures. What did they enjoy the most? What else would they have liked to see or do? How did they show distance in their picture? Where did they create texture?

Share Time/Evaluation

_____

_____

_____

_____

Curriculum Connection

Science, Social Studies, Language Arts

Creative Playground

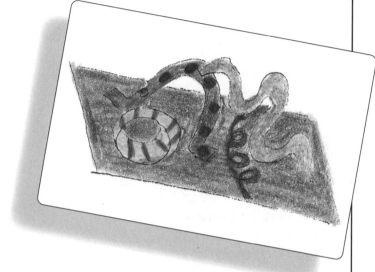

Objectives/Concepts

1. To work with line variety.
2. To experiment with abstract art.
3. To create three dimensions.
4. To work with layering.
5. To work with overlapping.
6. To experiment with folding, curling, and interlocking.
7. To create patterns.
8. To experiment with sculpture.
9. To experiment with cutting and pasting.

Technique

Sculpture, Cutting and Pasting

Materials

9 in. x 12 in. black construction paper
Colored paper strips in a variety of
   lengths and thicknesses

Paper punch
Scissors
Glue

Alternate Materials

Variety of papers, stick-on stars or other shapes, colored markers, glitter, fancy-edged scissors

Activities/Process

1. Discuss and view visuals of playgrounds.
2. Discuss architecture as a form of art.
3. Glue one end of a colored strip to the black paper.
4. Bend, fold, or curve the strip before gluing the other end to the black paper.
5. Continue gluing strips to the black paper in a variety of ways. Holes can be punched out of some strips or punched circles can be added to other strips to create a pattern. Strips can be cut thinner and glued on top of other strips before gluing to the black paper. Stripes can be added to the strips. Zigzag, wavy, or curved edges can be cut from the strips. Strips can go over or under each other in an interlocking or inter-twining fashion.

Questions for Discussion

What is architecture? What does three dimensional mean? Have you ever been to a creative playground? What are some of the things that you can do there? What types of slides have you been on? Did you go through a tunnel? What form is a tunnel? Did you make any patterns on your strips? How did you change some of the strips? Tell me about your playground.

Share Time/Evaluation

Curriculum Connection

Social Studies, Language Arts, Math

Paper Bag House

Objectives/Concepts

1. To work with line, shape, and color.
2. To create texture.
3. To experiment with three dimensions.
4. To experiment with cutting and pasting technique.
5. To work with layering.
6. To work with overlapping.

Technique

Sculpture, Cutting and Pasting

Materials

Lunch-size paper bag
Newspapers
Stapler
6 in. x 8 in. black paper
Colored paper
Scissors
Glue

Alternate Materials

Colored markers, variety of papers

Activities/Process

1. Discuss and show visuals of houses.
2. Fill paper bag ¾ full with newspaper.
3. Fold top of paper bag over and over until it rests right above the stuffed part.
4. Fold black paper in half lengthwise.
5. Place folded paper over the top of the bag and staple it on to resemble a roof.
6. With colored paper, cut and glue doors, windows, shutters, mailbox, trees, flowers, etc. Remember to decorate all sides of the house.

Questions for Discussion

Did you make your house, a house you have seen, or did you imagine a house? What are the important parts of a house? Do you have anything coming out away from the house? Did you create texture anywhere on your house? Did you make a pattern anywhere? Who do you think might live in your house?

Share Time/Evaluation

_____

_____

_____

_____

Curriculum Connection

Science, Social Studies, Language Arts

Tree Mosaic

Objectives/Concepts

1. To work with line, shape, and color.
2. To work with contour.
3. To experiment with mosaic.
4. To work with layering.
5. To work with overlapping.
6. To experiment with cutting and pasting.

Technique

Cutting and Pasting

Materials

12 in. x 18 in. blue paper
12 in. x 18 in. black paper
9 in. x 12 in. black paper
9 in. x 12 in. dark green paper
½ in. x 12 in. strips of
   brown paper

½ in. x 12 in. strips of
   light green paper
Scissors
Glue
Paper punch

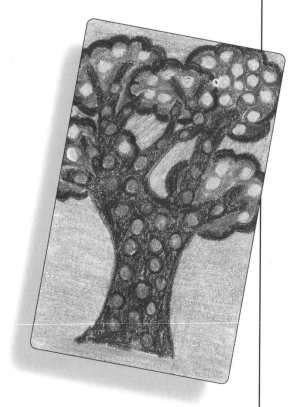

Alternate Materials

Colored markers, variety of papers, seeds, beans

Activities/Process

1. On 12 x 18 black paper, draw a tree that touches the edges of the paper.
2. Cut and glue the tree onto the blue paper.
3. With brown paper strips, punch out circles and glue them onto the tree, filling in the shape but leaving some black showing around each dot.
4. Using the dark green paper, cut some large curved shapes to represent clusters of leaves.
5. Glue the dark green shapes to the black paper. Leaving an edge about ¼ in., cut around the contour so that the black looks like an outline.
6. Glue onto the tops of the branches.
7. Punch out light green dots and glue onto the clusters of leaves.

Questions for Discussion

What is mosaic? How did you layer your paper? Do you have any overlapping in your picture? What are the parts of a tree and how do they relate to each other?

Share Time/Evaluation

_____
_____
_____
_____

Curriculum Connection

Science, Social Studies, Math

One-Point Perspective

Objectives/Concepts

1. To work with color, shape, and line.
2. To experiment with one-point perspective.
3. To work in silhouette.
4. To create distance.
5. To use warm colors.
6. To experiment with painting technique.
7. To experiment with drawing technique.

Technique

Painting, Drawing

Materials

8 in. x 11 in. watercolor paper
Fine-line permanent marker
Watercolor paints
Pencil
Ruler
Eraser

Alternate Materials

Colored chalk

Activities/Process

1. Discuss and show visuals of streets or roads diminishing into the distance.
2. Discuss and show visuals of trees.
3. Put a small dot with pencil in the middle of the paper.
4. From each of the bottom corners draw a light line to the dot, creating a triangle.
5. Paint a sky with watercolors, with blended colors representing the sunset. Start at the top of the paper and paint all the space except for the triangle.
6. Paint the triangle black.
7. Lightly draw lines from the two top corners to the point in the middle.
8. With black marker draw the shapes of trees reaching from the lines to the triangle on both sides. The trees closest to the sides of the paper will be taller than the trees closest to the point.

Questions for Discussion

If you are on a road and look into the distance, what happens to the road? What happens to the trees along the edge of the road? What is silhouette? What are considered warm colors? What is one-point perspective?

Share Time/Evaluation

_____

_____

_____

Curriculum Connection

Science, Math

Jungle or Rain Forest Scene

Objectives/Concepts

1. To work with line and shape.
2. To blend and mix colors.
3. To create a variety of greens.
4. To work with overlapping.
5. To create texture.
6. To create density.
7. To experiment with painting technique.
8. To experiment with drawing technique.

Technique

Drawing, Painting

Materials

12 in. x 18 in. white paper
Black crayon
Watercolor paints

Alternate Materials

Crayons (wax or oil), tempera paint, assorted colored paper, variety of papers, yarn

Activities/Process

1. Discuss and show visuals of jungles or rain forests.
2. With black crayon draw a jungle scene, filling in the paper. Overlap to create a feeling of density.
3. Paint in with watercolor paints, mixing and blending colors to make a variety of greens.

Questions for Discussion

What might you find in a jungle or rainforest? What does dense mean and how can we create a feeling of density? How do we make the color green? How do the greens in your painting differ? How did you show texture in your picture?

Share Time/Evaluation

_____
_____
_____
_____

Curriculum Connection

Science, Social Studies

Straw-Blown-Paint Tree

Objectives/Concepts

1. To work with line, shape, and color.
2. To create texture.
3. To experiment with painting technique.
4. To experiment with printing technique.

Technique

Painting, Printing

Materials

9 in. x 12 in. white paper
Watered-down brown tempera paint
Watercolor paints
Q-tips
Drinking straw

Alternate Materials

1 in. x 1 in. sponges, colored tempera paint, crayons (wax or oil), assorted colored papers, scissors, glue

Activities/Process

1. Discuss and view visuals of trees and leaves.
2. Drip some watered-down brown paint on the white paper.
3. With the straw close to the paint, blow the paint in an upward direction.
4. As the paint separates, blow in upward and outward directions to create branches and limbs.
5. Paint grass, rocks, flowers, etc. around the tree.
6. With the Q-tip, print dots for leaves in fall colors.

Questions for Discussion

What are the parts of a tree? How does a tree grow? Which direction are the branches on your tree growing? Was it hard to make the paint go where you wanted it to? What is the difference between painting and printing? How did you show texture? What makes your tree seem poetic?

Share Time/Evaluation

_____
_____
_____
_____

Curriculum Connection

Science, Social Studies, Language Arts

Winter Tree

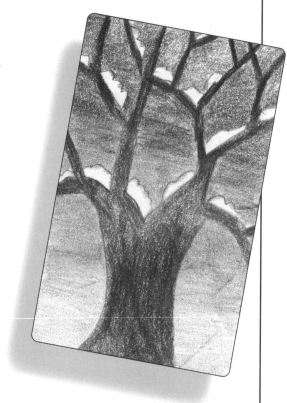

Objectives/Concepts
1. To work with shape and color.
2. To work with tint and shade.
3. To experiment with monochromatic color.
4. To create texture.
5. To experiment with painting technique.

Technique
Painting

Materials
12 in. x 18 in. white or manila paper
Tempera paints (blue, white, and black)
10 in. x 16 in. brown or black construction paper
Cotton or fiberfill
Glue

Alternate Materials
Watercolor paints, oil crayons

Activities/Process
1. Discuss and view visuals of skies and trees.
2. Paint the entire paper blue. Begin at the top, mixing blue with black to make a darker blue. Use less black as the paint reaches the middle of the paper. Then add a little white to the blue to lighten the color, adding more white as the paint reaches the bottom of the page.
3. While the paint is drying, draw and cut a tree from the construction paper, large enough that the branches go all the way to the edges of the paper.
4. Glue over the painted sky.
5. Glue little bits of cotton or fiberfill to the tree branches to represent snow.

Questions for Discussion
Why does a sky look darker and lighter? What does monochromatic mean? How do we make a shade of a color? How do we make a tint of a color? What are the parts of a tree and how do their sizes compare to each other? Why aren't there any leaves on the tree? After a snowstorm why might there be snow on the tree?

Share Time/Evaluation
_____
_____
_____
_____

Curriculum Connection
Science, Social Studies

Crayon-Resist Fall Tree

Objectives/Concepts

1. To work with line, shape, and color.
2. To experiment with crayon resist.
3. To work with silhouette.
4. To experiment with drawing technique.
5. To experiment with painting technique.

Technique

Painting

Materials

12 in. x 18 in. white paper
Black oil crayon
Watered-down tempera paint (orange)

Alternate Materials

Crayons (wax or oil), watered-down blue tempera paint, watercolor paint

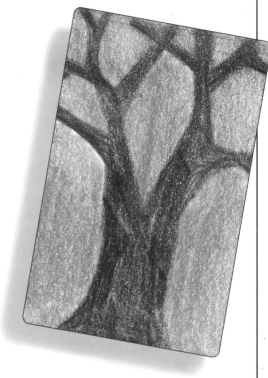

Activities/Process

1. Discuss and view visuals on trees.
2. With black crayon, draw a large tree. Bear down hard to make the tree dark. Have the tree branches touch the edges of the paper.
3. Paint over the tree, filling in the entire paper.
4. Wipe the entire paper gently with a paper towel to remove excess paint.

Questions for Discussion

Why didn't the paint hide the crayon tree? What are the parts of a tree? What is different about the size of branches, limbs, and twigs? What happens to the leaves in the fall? What time of year is it when the colorful leaves fall off the tree? Do all trees lose their leaves?

Share Time/Evaluation

_____
_____
_____
_____

Curriculum Connection

Science, Social Studies

Long Tree

Objectives/Concepts

1. To work with line, shape, and color.
2. To work with positive and negative shapes.
3. To work with overlapping.
4. To create a silhouette.
5. To work with contour edge.
6. To experiment with drawing technique.

Technique

Drawing

Materials

9 in. x 24 in. black paper
Colored chalk

Alternate Materials

Oil crayons

Activities/Process

1. Discuss and view visuals of trees.
2. With white chalk draw a tree. Start at the bottom of the paper and go all the way to the top of the paper. The branches should touch the edge of the paper.
3. In the negative spaces formed, leave about ¼ inch of black showing and make the contour edge of the negative shape with a different color of chalk.
4. Fill in the contour shapes with colored chalk.

Questions for Discussion

What is the thickest part of a tree? What happens to the thickness as the branches get farther from the trunk? Where might we find trees of this type? What shapes did you create in the negative spaces? Did you run into any problems with the chalk? What did you have to be careful of?

Share Time/Evaluation

_____
_____
_____
_____

Curriculum Connection

Science, Social Studies

Forest Trees

Objectives/Concepts

1. To work with line, shape, and size.
2. To work with variations of the same color.
3. To work with repetition.
4. To work with overlapping.

Technique

Cutting and Pasting

Materials

12 in. x 18 in. black paper
4½ in. x 6 in. variety of green-colored papers
4½ in. x 6 in. variety of brown-colored
    papers
Scissors
Glue

Alternate Materials

Variety of papers

Activities/Process

1. Discuss and view visuals of trees and forests.
2. Create a variety of trees using different shades of green. Make triangles of different sizes, then glue them on top of each other. Fold the green paper and cut a zigzag line from one corner diagonally to the other side. Cut a large triangle and then cut small negative triangles away from the edges or fringe them.
3. Brown squares and rectangles can be used for tree trunks or can be made into trees by gluing rectangles of varying thicknesses together.
4. Glue trees to the black paper, overlapping to create the feel of a forest.

Questions for Discussion

What is a forest? How are trees similar? How are they different? What are some different ways that you can make trees? Where did you overlap? How are the green colors different?

Share Time/Evaluation

_____
_____
_____
_____

Curriculum Connection

Science, Social Studies, Math

Scratch Art Tree

Objectives/Concepts

1. To work with silhouette.
2. To use positive and negative space.
3. To experiment with etching.

Technique

Drawing

Materials

Scratch art paper (multicolored)
Wooden scratch tool

Alternate Materials

Oak tag, oil crayons, black paint or ink

Activities/Process

1. Discuss and view trees.
2. Draw a tree shape with the wooden tool.
3. Scratch off the negative spaces around the tree to expose the colors underneath, leaving the tree as a black silhouette.

Questions for Discussion

How are trees similar? How are they different? What is a silhouette? What happened when you scratched off the black areas? How is this like etching?

Share Time/Evaluation

_____
_____
_____
_____

Curriculum Connection

Science, Social Studies

Positive and Negative Tree Design

Objectives/Concepts

1. To work with line and shape.
2. To work with silhouette.
3. To work with repetition.
4. To create overlapping.
5. To work with positive and negative space.

Technique

Drawing, Cutting and Pasting

Materials

12 in. x 18 in. white drawing paper	Scissors
4½ in. x 6 in. oak tag	Pencil
4½ in. x 6 in. brown paper	Glue
Brown and green fine-line markers	Scissors

Alternate Materials

4½ in. x 6 in. black paper, fine black marker, colored pencils

Activities/Process

1. Discuss and view trees.
2. Draw a tree on the oak tag.
3. Cut out the tree and use it as a stencil to cut a tree out of the brown paper.
4. Glue the brown tree anywhere on the white paper.
5. Using the brown marker trace the oak tag tree several times on the paper so that the edges touch each other or overlap. The trees must also touch the edges of the paper.
6. In the negative spaces that have been formed, draw a green line around the edges. Continue drawing lines inside these lines leaving only a small space between the lines. The lines can be thick or thin for variety.

Questions for Discussion

What is silhouette? How are trees similar? How are they different? What is positive and negative space? Where did you overlap?

Share Time/Evaluation

_____
_____
_____
_____

Curriculum Connection

Science, Social Studies

Styrofoam Printed Leaves

Objectives/Concepts

1. To work with line, shape, and color.
2. To experiment with printing technique.
3. To work with overlapping.
4. To create texture.
5. To work with repetition.
6. To experiment with color mixing.

Technique

Printing

Materials

12 in. x 18 in. light-colored paper
Thin Styrofoam
Leaves
Printing ink, printing plate, brayer
Pencil
Scissors

Alternate Materials

Tempera paint, brushes

Activities/Process

1. Discuss and view real leaves.
2. Trace a leaf onto the Styrofoam with the pencil.
3. Cut out the leaf. Add veins by pressing into the Stryrofoam with a pencil.
4. At a printing station (a table or group of desks covered with newspaper), roll the printing ink onto the printing plate until there is a thin smooth coating.
5. Roll the brayer over the Styrofoam leaf on the vein side.
6. At a clean desk, place the Styrofoam leaf print-side down onto the paper. Turn over and rub with the palm of your hand over the leaf. Lift up leaf and repeat the process using different colors. Students can share leaves for variety. Leaves can be overlapped. Print several times until the paper is filled with leaves.

Questions for Discussion

What are veins on a leaf? Why do leaves change color? How are leaves alike? How are leaves different? Are leaves all the same on one particular tree? What is a print? What happened if you did not bear down hard with the pencil and the line did not go below the surface? What if you used too much ink and did not roll the ink thin? Could you print the same leaf more than one time?

Share Time/Evaluation

_____
_____
_____

Curriculum Connection

Science, Social Studies

Textured Leaves with Bugs

Objectives/Concepts

1. To work with line, shape, and color.
2. To create texture.
3. To work with overlapping.
4. To experiment with the printing process of texture rubbing.
5. To experiment with cutting and pasting technique.

Technique

Cutting and Pasting, Printing

Materials

12 in. x 18 in. white paper
4½ in. x 6 in. green, brown, red, yellow, and orange paper
Assorted scraps of colored paper
Real leaves
Crayons (wax or oil)
Scissors
Glue

Alternate Materials

Various papers, felt, craft eyes, pipe cleaners, markers

Activities/Process

1. Discuss and view real leaves.
2. Discuss and view visuals of bugs.
3. Make a texture rubbing of a leaf by placing the leaf under the white paper and coloring over it with crayon.
4. Make several rubbings of leaves all over the paper.
5. Using the colored paper, trace a few real leaves and cut them out.
6. Add the veins with crayon.
7. Glue these paper leaves all over the paper. Overlap some of them and some of the texture-rubbed leaves.
8. Make bugs out of the colored scraps and glue onto some of the leaves.

Questions for Discussion

Why do leaves change color? What is similar about leaves? What is different about leaves? How did you overlap? Why can we see the shape and texture of the crayon rubbed leaves? Why is texture rubbing a form of printing?

Share Time/Evaluation

_____

_____

_____

Curriculum Connection

Science, Social Studies

Chalk-Line Leaves

Objectives/Concepts

1. To use line, shape, and color.
2. To create patterns.
3. To use repetition.
4. To create texture.
5. To overlap.
6. To be able to trace a shape.

Technique

Drawing

Materials

12 in. x 18 in. dark blue construction paper
Colored chalk
Oak tag stencil leaves

Alternate Materials

Colored markers, oil or wax crayons, colored pencils

Activities/Process

1. Observe and discuss real leaves.
2. Point out the veins on the leaves.
3. Demonstrate how to trace the leaf-shaped oak tag using different colors of chalk.
4. Trace many leaves and have some overlap.
5. Fill in the leaves with colored chalk lines to represent the veins.

Questions for Discussion

What do you notice about leaves? Are leaves perfect shapes? Why are there vein lines on leaves? Why do leaves change color? When leaves fall to the ground how can we tell which leaf is on top of another leaf?

Share Time/Evaluation

_____
_____
_____
_____

Curriculum Connection

Science, Social Studies

Watercolor Leaves

Objectives/Concepts

1. To use line, shape, and color.
2. To create patterns.
3. To use repetition.
4. To be able to trace a shape.

Technique

Drawing, Painting

Materials

12 in. x 18 in. white drawing paper
Oak tag stencil leaves
Black crayon
Watercolor paints

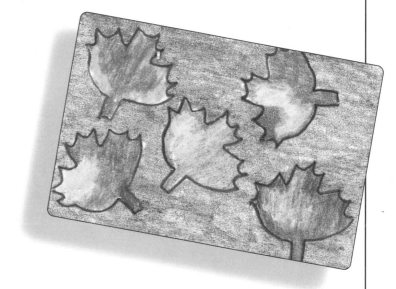

Alternate Materials

Markers, colored pencils, oil crayons, tempera paints

Activities/Process

1. Discuss and view real leaves.
2. Trace oak tag leaves several times on the white paper with the black crayon. Press hard to make the line dark.
3. Paint inside the leaves using one or more colors except black, blue, and purple.
4. Using blue and purple, paint all around the leaves.

Questions for Discussion

How are leaves similar? How are they different? Why do leaves change color? What happened if you used a lot of water on your brush? What happened if you didn't have enough water?

Share Time/Evaluation

_____
_____
_____

_____

Curriculum Connection

Science, Social Studies

Positive and Negative Leaves Design

Objectives/Concepts

1. To use line and color.
2. To create patterns.
3. To reinforce fine motor skills through tracing.
4. To overlap.
5. To work with positive and negative shapes.

Technique

Drawing

Materials

12 in. x 18 in. drawing paper
Leaves
Oak tag
Scissors
Colored markers

Alternate Materials

Crayons (wax or oil), colored pencils

Activities/Process

1. View and discuss leaves.
2. Trace real leaves onto oak tag and cut out for stencils.
3. Trace oak tag leaves onto white paper with black marker. Leaves need to be touching each other or the edges of the paper. Some can be overlapped.
4. Draw veins inside the leaves.
5. In the negative spaces created, make patterns with various colors.

Questions for Discussion

What are veins and why do leaves have them? Why do leaves change color? How are the leaves similar? How are they different? Point out your favorite pattern. Explain what a negative and positive space is and give an example.

Share Time/Evaluation

_____
_____
_____
_____

Curriculum Connection

Science, Social Studies, Math

Silhouette with Crayon-Resist Design

Objectives/Concepts

1. To work with line, shape, and color.
2. To work with silhouette.
3. To create pattern.
4. To work with repetition.
5. To experience color mixing.
6. To experiment with painting technique.
7. To experiment with crayon resist.

Technique

Cutting and Pasting, Drawing, Painting

Materials

12 in. x 18 in. white paper
4½ in. x 6 in. black paper
Scissors
Glue
Crayons (wax or oil)
Watercolor paints

Alternate Materials

Tempera paints, Colored paper

Activities/Evaluation

1. Discuss and show visuals of whatever subject matter is being reinforced in the curriculum, such as trees, flowers, birds, or animals.
2. Cut out the shape of the silhouette from the black paper. Glue to the bottom of the white paper.
3. Leaving some space around the silhouette, follow the contour and draw black lines about 1 inch apart. Repeat until all the paper is covered.
4. With crayons, make patterns inside each strip.
5. Paint each strip with watercolor paints, going right over the crayon marks.

Questions for Discussion

What is a silhouette? What is contour? What type of patterns did you make? What did you repeat? Did you make any colors by mixing other colors? Why didn't the paint hide the crayon marks?

Share Time/Evaluation

_____

_____

_____

Curriculum Connection

Science, Math

Flower Garden

Objectives/Concepts

1. To work with line, shape, and color.
2. To work with detail.
3. To work with overlapping.
4. To create texture.
5. To work with layering.

Technique

Cutting and Pasting

Materials

12 in. x 18 in. blue paper
4½ in. x 6 in. assorted colored papers
3 in. x 9 in. variety of green colored papers
Scissors
Glue

Alternate Materials

Variety of papers, buttons, beads, glitter

Activities/Process

1. Discuss and view visuals of flowers and flower gardens.
2. Cut a variety of shapes for flowers. If making more than one petal the same, cut several at the same time by stacking the paper before cutting.
3. Glue shapes together to resemble different types of flowers.
4. Glue to stems. Add leaves to stems.
5. Glue flowers to blue paper, overlapping some of them. Add grass, bugs, etc.

Questions for Discussion

What shapes did you use to create some of your flowers? Where did you use layering? Where did you overlap? How are the shades of green different? How did you make your grass?

Share Time/Evaluation

_____
_____
_____
_____

Curriculum Connection

Science, Social Studies, Math

Flower Transfer Drawing

Objectives/Concepts

1. To work with line, shape, and color.
2. To create a transfer drawing.
3. To experiment with making a copy or print.

Technique

Drawing, Printmaking

Materials

9 in. x 12 in. white drawing paper
Oil crayons
Pencil
Black fine-line marker

Alternate Materials

Wax crayons

Activities/Process

1. Discuss and view visuals of flowers (birds, insects, or other subjects could be used as well).
2. Fold paper in half crosswise.
3. Open the paper and color one half of the paper, using oil crayons in a variety of colors. Color dark and smooth.
4. Fold the paper and draw on the backside of the colored part with the pencil. Draw large and dark. Fill in the shapes with the pencil to transfer the color. Do not just outline as there will not be much to transfer.
5. Open the paper and outline the transferred shapes with the fine-line black marker.

Questions for Discussion

What does transfer mean? Did you color and draw dark enough to make a good transfer or do you think you need to go over it again? What makes your colored print the same as the original drawing? How is it different?

Share Time/Evaluation

_____
_____
_____
_____

Curriculum Connection

Science

Flower Print

Objectives/Concepts

1. To work with line, shape, and color.
2. To work with repetition.
3. To create pattern.
4. To create texture.
5. To work with layering.
6. To work with overlapping.
7. To experience color mixing.
8. To experiment with printing techniques.

Technique

Printing

Materials

12 in. x 18 in. colored paper
Tempera paint
Brushes
Scraps and gadgets (wood pieces, film covers, spools, sponges, cardboard pieces)

Alternate Materials

Stamp ink pads

Activities/Process

1. Discuss and view visuals of flowers.
2. Paint the edge or flat part of an object and press onto the paper.
3. Repeat painting and pressing either the same object or different objects, in order to make the shape of a flower.
4. Continue making flowers until the paper is full.
5. Strips of cardboard or craft sticks can be used to make grass.

Questions for Discussion

What are some of the gadgets you used to make the shapes of parts of your flowers? What is the difference between painting and printing? Does the texture of the gadget you used show up on the paper? What happened if you used too much paint on the gadget? What happened when you printed the gadget several times before painting again? Did you mix colors to make new colors? What colors did you make?

Share Time/Evaluation

_____

_____

_____

_____

Curriculum Connection

Science, Math

Clay Bugs

Objectives/Concepts

1. To work with color, line, and pattern.
2. To work with symmetry.
3. To create three dimensions.
4. To experiment with sculpture technique.
5. To experiment with clay.

Technique

Sculpture, Drawing, Cutting

Materials

Clay (about the size of a tennis ball)
3 in. x 4 in. white oak tag (2 pieces)
Colored markers
Scissors
Pipe cleaners
Toothpick or pointed craft stick

Alternate Materials

Glitter, crayons, small buttons, beads, craft eyes

Activities/Process

1. Discuss and view visuals of bugs.
2. Holding two white oak tag papers together, cut out the shape of a bug's wings.
3. With colored markers, draw a pattern on the wings so they are exactly the same on both wings.
4. Form the body and head of the bug by pinching, pulling, or joining the clay.
5. Push wings into the clay body.
6. Add antennae and legs with cut pipe cleaners.
7. Make details with toothpick or pointed craft stick.

Questions for Discussion

What is the difference between a bug and an insect? What is symmetry? Are the patterns on your bug's wings symmetrical? What type of pattern or design did you use? How did you make the body of your bug?

Share Time/Evaluation

_____

_____

_____

_____

Curriculum Connection

Science, Social Studies, Math

Looking in the Grass with a Magnifying Glass

Objectives/Concepts

1. To work with line, shape, and color.
2. To work with detail.
3. To create overlapping.
4. To create texture.
5. To work with magnification.
6. To experiment with drawing technique.

Technique

Drawing

Materials

12 in. x 18 in. white paper
3 in. circle pattern to trace
Assorted colored markers
½ in. x 6 in. strip of black paper
Crayons (wax)

Alternate Materials

Watercolor paints, oil crayons, colored pencils, assorted colored construction paper

Activities/Process

1. Discuss and view visuals of grass, flowers, and bugs.
2. Trace the circle with black marker.
3. Glue black strip touching the circle, to resemble a magnifying glass.
4. Fill in entire paper except inside the circle with a crayon drawing of grass, flowers, rocks, bugs, and whatever we might find in the grass.
5. Continue the drawing inside the circle with colored markers, making the grass, bugs, etc. larger than the outside crayon drawing.

Questions for Discussion

What might we find in the grass? How are the shades of green different? What is a magnifying glass? What happens to color under a magnifying glass? How did you show texture? What makes the picture seem close up?

Share Time/Evaluation

_____
_____
_____
_____

Curriculum Connection

Science

Caterpillars on Leaves

Objectives/Concepts

1. To work with color and shape.
2. To experiment with watercolor techniques.
3. To experience folding to create movement.

Technique

Painting, Cutting and Pasting

Materials

3 in. diameter precut white circles (6 per child)
12 in. x 18 in. green paper
¼ in. x 3 in. black strips (10 per child)
1 in. black squares (2 per child)
Watercolor paints
Glue
Scissors

Alternate Materials

crayons (wax or oil), chalk, pastels, colored construction paper scraps

Activities/Process

1. Discuss and show visuals of caterpillars and leaves.
2. Cut one large leaf from green paper. Cut into the edges to illustrate where the leaf might have been nibbled on.
3. Paint the 6 circles with watercolors.
4. Glue the circles together to form the body of the caterpillar.
5. Fold the strips for the legs back and forth, like an accordian. Glue on legs and antennae.
6. Round the squares to make eyes. Glue down.
7. Glue caterpillar to the leaf.

Questions for Discussion

What do you know about caterpillars? How did you glue the circles together to make the body look like it was bending? What happened with the wet watercolors when the colors touched each other? How did folding the paper strip change the line?

Share Time/Evaluation

_____
_____
_____
_____

Curriculum Connection

Science, Math

Crayon Bugs with
Watercolor Leaves

Objectives/Concepts

1. To work with line, shape, color, and texture.
2. To create different shades of green.
3. To experience crayon resist.
4. To experience watercolor painting.

Technique

Drawing, Painting

Materials

9 in. x 12 in. white paper
Crayons
Watercolor paints

Alternate Materials

Colored pencils, construction paper, colored chalk, pastels

Activities/Process

1. Discuss and view visuals of bugs.
2. Discuss and view visuals of grass.
3. Draw bugs of various sizes, shapes, and colors.
4. Using a black crayon, draw the outline of leaves and grass around the bugs.
5. Paint in the leaves and grass using different shades of green.

Questions for Discussion

What can you tell me about bugs? Where do they live? What color are they? Is grass all the same color? How do we make different kinds of green? What happened when you painted over the bugs? How many bugs do you have hiding in the grass?

Share Time/Evaluation

_____
_____
_____
_____

Curriculum Connection

Science, Language Arts, Math

Bugs in a Container

Objectives/Concepts

1. To use line, shape, and color.
2. To create detail.
3. To enlarge.
4. To overlap.

Technique

Drawing

Materials

9 in. x 12 in. white paper
Precut construction paper lid, cut from
    4 in. x 12 in. paper
Black marker
Crayons
Glue

Alternate Materials

Colored pencils, watercolor paints, colored markers

Activities/Process

1. Look at books about insects.
2. Gather leaves, rocks, grass, and insects in a container.
3. Observe the details and discuss.
4. With black marker, draw one or more insects, grass, leaves, etc.
5. Color in with crayons.
6. Glue construction paper lid to the top of the white paper.

Questions for Discussion

What can you tell me about an insect? Where do we find insects? What kind of shapes are insects? Is all grass the same color? What did you find in your clump of grass?

Share Time/Evaluation

Curriculum Connection

Science, Math

Textured Mountains

Objectives/Concepts

1. To work with color and shape.
2. To experience texture rubbing.
3. To experiment with printing technique.
4. To work with overlapping.
5. To create distance.
6. To work with foreground, middle ground, and background.

Technique

Cutting and Pasting, Printing

Materials

9 in. x 2 in. blue paper
3 in. x 12 in. green paper
Assorted green paper scraps
Brown paper scraps
4½ in. x 6 in. white paper
   (several pieces)
Assorted
   textures on
   flat surfaces
Crayons (wax or oil)
Scissors
Glue

Alternate Materials

Variety of colored papers, colored chalk

Activities/Process

1. Discuss and view visuals of mountains and trees.
2. Place a texture under a white paper and rub the flat part of a crayon back and forth, causing a texture to appear. Use several papers and create many rubbings in a variety of colors and textures.
3. Glue the green paper to the bottom of the blue paper.
4. Cut mountain shapes from the colored textured papers. Glue these down in the background by over-lapping them above the green paper.
5. With brown and green paper cut and glue tree shapes in the foreground and middle ground.
6. A sun or clouds can be added with colored scraps.

Questions for Discussion

What is texture? How did you create some of your textures? What did you do to create distance? What is in the foreground of your picture? How are your trees different?

Share Time/Evaluation

_____
_____
_____
_____

Curriculum Connection

Science, Social Studies, Math

Chalk Mountains

Objectives/Concepts

1. To work with outline.
2. To overlap triangular shapes.
3. To blend colors.
4. To experiment with colored chalk.

Technique

Drawing

Materials

12 in. x 18 in. white drawing paper
Black crayon
Colored chalk
Tissue

Alternate Materials

Crayons (oil or wax), watercolor paints, tempera paints

Activities/Process

1. View and discuss pictures of mountains.
2. Using black crayon, outline several overlapping triangular shapes.
3. Color in with a variety of colored chalk.
4. Blend colors with the tissue.

Questions for Discussion

What is a mountain? What gives mountains their colors? How did you get the colors in your mountains?
Which of your mountains seem farther away and why? Are mountains always pointed or can they be
rounded on the top?

Share Time/Evaluation

_____

_____

_____

_____

Curriculum Connections

Science, Social Studies, Math

Mountain Range

Objectives/Concepts

1. To work with color, shape, and line.
2. To create distance.
3. To work with patterns.
4. To experience crayon resist.
5. To experiment with watercolor technique.

Technique

Drawing, Painting

Materials

12 in. x 18 in. white paper
Crayons (wax or oil)
Watercolor paints

Alternate Materials

Chalk, pastel-colored pencils

Activities/Process

1. Discuss and show visuals of mountains.
2. On white paper with black crayon, start at the bottom and draw
   rounded or peaked mountain shapes. Have them touching each other.
3. Continue adding rows of mountain shapes until a little more than half the paper is filled.
4. Fill in each mountain with a pattern of lines and shapes in different colors.
5. A sun or clouds can be added to the sky.
6. Fill in with watercolor paints.

Questions for Discussion

What are mountains? How does a faraway mountain look different than a mountain that is closer to us? Which of your mountains are closer to the viewer? Point out your favorite pattern and tell us how you made it.

Share Time/Evaluation

_____
_____
_____
_____

Curriculum Connection

Science, Social Studies, Math

Volcano Explosions

Objectives/Concepts

1. To use line, color, and shape.
2. To create patterns.
3. To use repetition.
4. To show movement.

Technique

Drawing

Materials

12 in. x 18 in. black paper
11 in. x 17 in. white paper
Glue
Oil crayons
Scissors

Alternate Materials

Markers, colored chalk, tempera paint

Activities/Process

1. Discuss volcanoes, eruptions, and explosions.
2. With black oil crayon draw the shape of a mountain or volcano in the middle of the paper, going only about halfway to the top.
3. Color the shape.
4. Add another black line about two inches away from the first line. Use a wavy or bumpy line to show movement.
5. Color this area in or use short or zigzag lines to represent movement.
6. Continue adding lines and decorating until the top of the page.
7. Cut out the volcano shape.
8. Glue to the black paper.

Questions for Discussion

What is a volcano? What makes it erupt? What kind of lines did you use? How did you make it look as though your shape is exploding?

Share Time/Evaluation

_____
_____
_____
_____

Curriculum Connection

Science, Social Studies

Mountain Chalk Rubbings

Objectives/Concepts

1. To work with line and shape.
2. To work with contour.
3. To experiment with color mixing.
4. To work with overlapping.
5. To experiment with cutting.
6. To experiment with printing technique.

Technique

Cutting, Printing

Materials

18 in. x 12 in. white paper
6 in. x 18 in. oak tag (3 per child)
Scissors
Colored chalk
Facial tissue

Alternate Materials

12 in. x 18 in. colored paper, pastels

Activities/Process

1. Discuss and view visuals of mountain ranges.
2. Cut a line to resemble a mountain range on the long side of one piece of oak tag.
3. Color the top half of the oak tag with colored chalk.
4. Place the oak tag 4 or 5 inches from the top of the white paper.
5. Rub over the chalk with tissue, brushing the excess chalk onto the white paper.
6. Repeat this process using another piece of oak tag. Move the oak tag down each time to expose more white paper.
7. Continue using pieces of oak tag again and again until the entire paper is filled with colorful mountain images.

Questions for Discussion

What is a mountain range? Why do mountains appear to be different colors? How did you blend some of your colors? Are the tops of mountains always pointed? What type of line did you use to make the contour of the mountaintops?

Share Time/Evaluation

_____
_____
_____
_____

Curriculum Connection

Science, Social Studies

Constellations

Objectives/Concepts

1. To work with shape.
2. To work with contour.
3. To work with silhouette.
4. To work with repetition.
5. To experiment with cutting and pasting technique.

Technique

Cutting and Pasting

Materials

12 in. x 18 in. black paper
12 in. x 18 in. dark blue paper
Scraps of yellow paper
Scraps of white paper
Circle paper punch
Star paper punch
Glue
Scissors

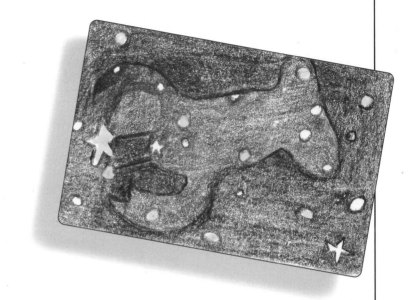

Alternate Materials

Tempera paint (white and yellow), Q-tip, stick-on stars

Activities/Process

1. Discuss and view visuals of stars and constellations.
2. Cut a large shape for a constellation (animal, person, etc.) out of the dark blue paper.
3. Glue onto the black paper.
4. Punch circles and stars from white and yellow paper. Glue them inside and outside the silhouette shape, making sure some of them form part of the contour.

Questions for Discussion

What is a star? What is a constellation? Why do you think there are constellations? Why do the positions of stars change? What makes some stars seem brighter than others? What makes some stars seem larger than others?

Share Time/Evaluation

_____
_____
_____
_____

Curriculum Connection

Science, Social Studies, Math, Language Arts

Star Gazers

Objectives/Concepts

1. To work with line and shape.
2. To create texture.
3. To create pattern.
4. To show distance.
5. To experiment with drawing technique.
6. To experiment with cutting and pasting technique.
7. To experiment with printing technique.
8. To work with a viewpoint from behind.

Technique

Drawing, Cutting and Pasting, Printing

Materials

12 in. x 18 in. black paper	Glue
12 in. x 18 in. white paper	White tempera paint
Black marker	Toothpick
Crayons (wax or oil)	Q-tip
Scissors	

Alternate Materials

Yellow tempera paint, stick-on stars, assorted colors of construction paper, variety of papers, yarn, felt, fabric

Activities/Process

1. Discuss and view a nighttime sky with stars.
2. Discuss and view the backs of people's heads, noticing the style and texture of the hair.
3. On the white paper with a black marker draw the back of someone's head, neck, and shoulders. Add lines for the style and texture of the hair.
4. Make lines or shapes into a pattern on the clothing.
5. Color in with crayons, cut out and glue onto the bottom of the black paper (held vertically).
6. Using the Q-tip and toothpick, print white dots representing stars all around the head.

Questions for Discussion

What we would see at night in the sky? What makes stars look different? How did you create texture for the person's hair? What type of pattern did you make? Why do the stars look far away? Do some stars look closer than others and why?

Share Time/Evaluation

_____
_____
_____
_____

Curriculum Connection

Science, Social Studies, Language Arts

Chalk-Stenciled Stars

Objectives/Concepts

1. To work with a variety of sizes.
2. To work with overlapping.
3. To experience color mixing and blending.
4. To experiment with chalk.
5. To experiment with printing techniques.
6. To work with positive and negative shapes and space.
7. To work with repetition.

Technique

Printing

Materials

12 in. x 18 in. white paper

Precut, oak tag star stencils in a variety of sizes (both the positive star shape and the oak tag with the negative star space will be used)

Colored chalk

Tissues or toilet paper

Alternate Materials

Pastels, oil crayons

Activities/Process

1. Discuss and show visuals about stars.
2. Color around the edge of an oak tag star with one or more colors of chalk.
3. Place the star on the white paper. While holding it down, use the tissue to smudge the chalk away from the star.
4. Lift the chalk and a negative star shape with colored streaks around it will appear.
5. Use the oak tag piece with the negative star space by coloring with chalk around the edge of the negative space.
6. With tissue rub the chalk into the center of the space. This will create a positive star shape.
7. Repeat several times. Overlap some stars and use different color combinations until the paper has a balanced design.

Questions for Discussion

What is a negative shape? What is a positive shape? What colors have you blended? How did you balance your design? Do you have a favorite star? What is a star?

Share Time/Evaluation

_____

_____

_____

Curriculum Connection

Science, Math

Man in the Moon

Objectives/Concepts

1. To work with three dimensions.
2. To create a mobile.
3. To experiment with cutting and pasting techniques.
4. To work with shape and color.
5. To create a pattern.
6. To create texture.
7. To work with facial features.
8. To work with profile or side view.

Technique

Sculpture, Cutting and Pasting

Materials

A crescent shape cut from   Hole puncher
   12 in. x 18 in. white paper   Glue
Colored construction paper scraps   Scissors
Large star stencil   String

Alternate Materials

Glitter, various papers, fabric, or felt

Activities/Process

1. Discuss and show visuals of the moon.
2. On the crescent-shaped paper add facial features with construction paper. Cut two at the same time for both sides of the paper moon.
3. Add hair by fringing or curling paper.
4. Nightcaps or other details can be added.
5. Trace the star stencil on white or yellow paper and cut out.
6. Punch a hole in the top and bottom of the moon and on the top of the star.
7. Connect the star to the moon with a piece of string, allowing the star to hang.
8. Add string to the top hole in the moon for hanging the mobile.

Questions for Discussion

Why do we say there is a man in the moon? What makes the moon look different on different nights? Why are there different shapes to the moon? What is a mobile? What type of pattern did you use on the nightcap?

Share Time/Evaluation

_____
_____
_____
_____

Curriculum Connection

Science, Social Studies, Math

Sun Faces

Objectives/Concepts

1. To work with line, shape, and color.
2. To create a pattern.
3. To create a feeling or emotion with facial features.
4. To use warm and cool colors.
5. To experiment with watercolor technique.
6. To experience crayon resist.
7. To experience color mixing.

Technique

Drawing, Painting

Materials

12 in. x 12 in. white paper
Black crayon
Watercolor paints

Alternate Materials

Tempera paints, construction paper, crayons (wax or oil)

Activities/Process

1. Discuss and show visuals of the sun.
2. Discuss facial features and how they can express emotions.
3. Draw a large circle with black crayon. Add sunrays in a pattern, using triangles or ovals.
4. Draw a face in the circle.
5. Using warm colors (red, yellow, and orange) paint in the sun.
6. Paint the space around the sun with cool colors.

Questions for Discussion

What is the sun? How does it make us feel? Does the expression on your sun's face make us feel a certain way? How did you mix your colors?

Share Time/Evaluation

_____

_____

_____

_____

Curriculum Connection

Science, Math

Tessellation

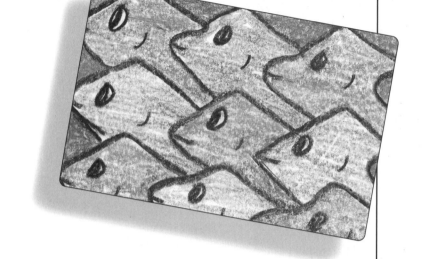

Objectives/Concepts

1. To work with tessellation.
2. To work with contour edge.
3. To work with repetition.
4. To experience watercolor technique.

Technique

Drawing, Cutting and Pasting, Painting

Materials

12 in. x 18 in. white paper
4 in. x 4 in. white paper
Scissors
Tape
Black crayon
Watercolor paints

Alternate Materials

Crayons (wax or oil), colored pencils

Activities/Process

1. Discuss and view visuals of tessellation.
2. On 4 in. x 4 in. paper, cut a curved or jagged section from the bottom and tape it to the top.
3. Cut a U shape or triangle shape from the right edge and tape it to the left edge.
4. With black crayon, trace this shape onto the large paper so it fits into itself like a puzzle piece, over and over again. Start on the top and go across the row. Then begin on the next row.
5. Paint in with watercolors. If the shape resembles something, small details, like eyes, can be added with black crayon.

Questions for Discussion

What is a tessellation? Did your shape resemble anything? What happened to the pieces that you cut away? Why does your pattern go on and on?

Share Time/Evaluation

_____
_____
_____
_____

Curriculum Connection

Math, Science

Quartered Fish

Objectives/Concepts

1. To work with color, shape, and line.
2. To create texture.
3. To create pattern.
4. To experience different art media.
5. To experiment with drawing technique.
6. To experiment with painting technique.

Technique

Drawing, Painting

Materials

12 in. x 12 in. white paper
Colored markers
Colored pencils
Crayons (wax or oil)
Watercolor paints

Alternate Materials

Assorted colors of construction paper, variety of papers, glitter, stick-on shapes, tempera paint

Activities/Process

1. Discuss and view visuals of fish.
2. Fold paper in half twice, to quarter the paper. Open the paper.
3. Draw a fish so that it has a part in each of the quartered pieces. Add weeds, rocks, and other objects to suggest an underwater environment.
4. Color one quarter with colored pencils.
5. Color another quarter with markers.
6. Color another quarter with watercolor paints.
7. Color the last quarter with crayons.

Questions for Discussion

What does quartered mean? What is multimedia? What does variation mean? How do the different materials make the picture look? Do you like one material better than another?

Share Time/Evaluation

_____

_____

_____

_____

Curriculum Connection

Science, Math

Tissue Paper Fish

Objectives/Concepts

1. To work with shape.
2. To work with overlapping.
3. To create texture.
4. To experiment with color blending.

Technique

Cutting and Pasting

Materials

12 in. x 18 in. white paper
1 in. squares of assorted colored tissue paper
Glue
Watered-down glue
Glue brushes
Assorted construction paper

Alternate Materials

Starch, gloss medium, variety of papers, craft eyes, buttons, glitter

Activities/Process

1. Discuss and view visuals of fish.
2. Cut a shape for the head of a fish from the construction paper. Add eyes and gills.
3. Cut shapes for the tail of a fish.
4. Glue the head and tail to the white paper, leaving room for the body.
5. Layer and overlap the 1 inch squares of tissue paper for the body of the fish, using watered-down glue and glue brushes.
6. Add fins with construction paper.

Questions for Discussion

What shape are fish? What is the difference between tissue paper and construction paper? What happened when two colors of tissue paper were layered or overlapped? What is the texture of a fish and how does your artwork show texture?

Share Time/Evaluation

_____
_____
_____

Curriculum Connection

Science, Social Studies

Fish Plaque

Objectives/Concepts

1. To work with line, shape, and color.
2. To create texture.
3. To experiment with clay.
4. To experiment with sculpture.
5. To work in relief.

Technique

Sculpture, painting

Materials

Self-hardening clay (size of a baseball)
Pointed craft stick
Toothpick
Paper clip
Watercolor paints

Alternate Materials

Tempera paints, acrylic paints, multicolor plasticine clay

Activities/Process

1. Discuss and view visuals of fish.
2. Press clay to flatten.
3. Cut a circle shape about 3 inches in diameter, using the craft stick.
4. With the leftover clay form the shape of a fish. Press and join to the plaque. Add details with toothpick.
5. Add rocks, weeds, and other objects made from clay to suggest a sea environment.
6. Paint with watercolors.
7. Push paperclip into the top of the clay for hanging the plaque when it is dry.

Questions for Discussion

What is relief? What would we find in an ocean environment? How did you make your fish? What do we need to do to join two pieces of clay together so they do not fall apart when they are dry? What did you have to be careful of when you painted?

Share Time/Evaluation

_____
_____
_____
_____

Curriculum Connection

Science, Social Studies

Depths of the Ocean

Objectives/Concepts

1. To create monochromatic color.
2. To work with tints and shades.
3. To experiment with painting techniques.
4. To experiment with cutting and pasting techniques.
5. To work with line, shape, and color.
6. To work with overlapping.
7. To create depth.

Technique

Painting, Cutting and Pasting

Materials

12 in. x 18 in. white or manila paper
Tempera paint (blue, black, and white)
Brushes
Paper towels
Construction paper scraps in a variety of colors
Glue
Scissors

Alternate Materials

Watercolor paints, variety of papers, sand, crayons, markers, colored pencils

Activities/Process

1. Discuss and view visuals about ocean life and environment.
2. Paint the depths of the ocean by mixing blue paint with white. Gradually change to all blue and then add black to make darker shades at the bottom of the paper.
3. With construction paper cut out ocean life, such as fish, rocks, weeds, crabs, etc.
4. Glue onto the painted ocean.

Questions for Discussion

What is the ocean and where are oceans located? What makes the color of the ocean change? What lives in the ocean? What is monochromatic? How did you mix your colors to make different tints and shades?

Share Time/Evaluation

_____
_____
_____
_____

Curriculum Connection

Science, Social Studies, Math

Aquarium Windsock

Objectives/Concepts

1. To work with line, shape, and color.
2. To work with overlapping.
3. To create texture.
4. To create pattern.
5. To experiment with crayon resist.
6. To experiment with drawing technique.
7. To experiment with painting technique.
8. To create a mobile.

Technique

Drawing, Painting

Materials

12 in. x 18 in. white paper
Crayons (wax or oil)
Watered-down blue tempera paint
Large brush
Paper towel
1 in. x 18 in. black strips
(2 per child)

18 in. blue crepe paper
strips (3 per child)
Paper punch
Stapler
String or yarn

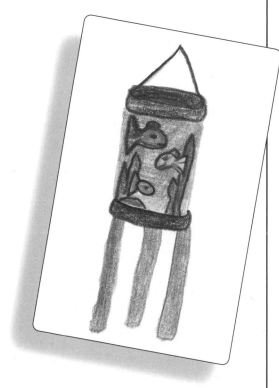

Alternate Materials

Plastic wrap, colored construction paper, glitter, watercolor paints

Activities/Process

1. Discuss and view visuals of fish, aquariums, and/or ocean environment.
2. With crayons draw an ocean scene with fish, weeds, rocks, etc. Make sure the drawing is dark.
3. With watered-down blue paint, paint over the entire picture.
4. Wipe carefully with a paper towel to remove extra paint.
5. When dry, glue or staple the black strips to the top and bottom of the picture.
6. Curl the paper into a cylinder and staple it.
7. Staple the crepe paper to the bottom of the cylinder.
8. Punch two holes opposite each other in the top and attach string or yarn for hanging.

Questions for Discussion

What shapes are fish? Where do fish live? What types of patterns did you use? Where did you overlap in your picture? What else did you add besides fish in your water scene? Have you ever seen or had an aquarium? Where else we would find fish? Are they always the same shape? What is a mobile? What form did we create by curling and stapling our paper?

Share Time/Evaluation

_____
_____
_____

Curriculum Connection

Science, Social Studies, Math

Sports Person

Objectives/Concepts

1. To work with line and shape.
2. To work with repetition.
3. To create movement.
4. To create pattern.
5. To work with contour.
6. To experiment with cutting and pasting technique.
7. To experiment with drawing technique.

Technique

Drawing, Cutting and Pasting

Materials

9 in. x 12 in. white paper   Glue
9 in. x 12 in. black paper   Black marker
Sports magazines   Ruler
Scissors

Alternate Materials

Colored markers, assorted colored paper, shaped stickers, variety of paper punches

Activities/Process

1. Discuss and show visuals of physical fitness and sports players in action.
2. Look through sports magazines and cut out a large picture of a sports player in an action shot.
3. Glue down on black paper and cut out, leaving a ¼-inch black border around the contour.
4. Glue down on the white paper.
5. With black marker draw a line following the contour of the black paper, about ¼ inch away.
6. Draw four or five more black contour lines around each previous line.
7. Draw a border around the edges of the paper with black marker.
8. Design inside the border with black marker, making lines, shapes, and patterns.

Questions for Discussion

What is physical fitness? What are some ways we can keep our bodies healthy? What kinds of sports do you like? How did you show movement in your picture? What type of pattern did you create? What is a contour line? How did the contour line change when it was repeated several times?

Share Time/Evaluation

_____
_____
_____
_____

Curriculum Connection

Science, Physical Education, Math

Self-Portrait

Objectives/Concepts

1. To work with line, shape, and color.
2. To work with layering and overlapping.
3. To work with texture through curling and fringing.
4. To work with facial features and proportion.
5. To experiment with cutting and pasting.

Technique

Cutting and Pasting

Materials

9 in. x 12 in. salmon, pink, eggshell, tan, or brown paper

4½ in. x 6 in. salmon, pink, eggshell, tan, or brown paper

3 in. x 4½ in. salmon, pink, eggshell, tan, or brown paper
   (3 per child)

3 in. x 4½ in. red paper

9 in. x 12 in. brown, yellow, black, or red paper

2 in. x 2 in. white paper (2 per child)

1½ in. x 1½ in. brown, blue, or green paper (2 per child)

1 in. x 1 in. black paper (2 per child)

4½ in. x 12 in. colored paper

Alternate Materials

Various papers, yarn, buttons, markers, crayons

Activities/Process

1. Discuss the importance of taking care of ourselves.
2. Discuss and view visuals of heads and facial features.
3. Round the edges of the 9 x 12 salmon, pink, eggshell, tan, or brown paper to make an oval for the face.
4. Add 4½ x 6 paper for the neck.
5. Layer two 3 x 4½ papers together, round two corners and glue on for the ears.
6. From the other 3 x 4½ paper, make a triangle and glue down for the nose.
7. Make a mouth out of the red paper by rounding the corners.
8. Round all small squares and layer them on top of each other for the eyes. Cut two of the same color at a time.
9. Make hair by cutting, curling, or fringing paper.
10. Round the two top corners of the 6 x 12 colored paper and glue to the neck for the shoulders.

Questions for Discussion

What is a self-portrait? How are people similar to each other? How are they different? How did you make the eyes and ears the same? How did you make the hair look like yours?

Share Time/Evaluation

_____

_____

Curriculum Connection

Science, Language Arts

Cylinder Characters

Objectives/Concepts

1. To work with shape and color.
2. To experiment with sculpture.
3. To create three dimensions.
4. To create texture.
5. To work with pattern.

Technique

Cutting and Pasting, Sculpture

Materials

4½ in. x 6 in. colored construction paper
Assorted colored paper scraps
Scissors
Glue
Markers

Alternate Materials

Yarn, fabric scraps, buttons, felt

Activities/Process

1. Discuss storybook characters or neighborhood helpers.
2. Form a cylinder by rolling the 4½ in. x 6 in. paper and gluing the short sides together.
3. Add scraps of paper to make clothing, buttons, belts, etc.
4. Cut, fringe, or curl paper for the hair.
5. Add facial features, hats, and other details.

Questions for Discussion

Who is your character? Tell us something about your character. How did you make the hair? Did you use a pattern in the clothing?

Share Time/Evaluation

_____
_____
_____
_____

Curriculum Connection

Language Arts, Social Studies

Faces in the Crowd

Objectives/Concepts

1. To work with line, shape, and color.
2. To work with overlapping.
3. To create pattern.
4. To create expression.
5. To experiment with watercolor technique.
6. To experiment with crayon resist.

Technique

Drawing, Painting

Materials

12 in. x 18 in. white paper
Crayons
Watercolor paints

Alternate Materials

Oil crayons, colored chalk, pastels, markers

Activities/Process

1. Discuss crowds of people and where they might be found.
2. Discuss facial features and hairstyles.
3. Beginning at the lower part of the paper, draw some circles or ovals to represent heads of people.
4. Under each circle or oval, draw curved lines to represent shoulders.
5. Draw some more circle heads higher on the page to be behind this group. Add curved shoulders on these also.
6. Add hair and facial features to show feelings and expressions.
7. Buttons and patterns can be added to the clothing.
8. Paint in with watercolors.

Questions for Discussion

Where do we see crowds of people? What kind of expressions would they have on their faces and why?
What happened when the paints went over the crayon? What types of patterns did you use?

Share Time/Evaluation

_____
_____
_____
_____

Curriculum Connection

Science, Language Arts

Neckties

Objectives/Concepts

1. To work with line, shape, and color.
2. To create pattern.
3. To work with clothing design.
4. To create texture.

Technique

Drawing

Materials

12 in. x 18 in. white paper
Colored markers
Crayons (wax or oil)

Alternate Materials

Colored papers, fabric, watercolor paints, tempera paints

Activities/Process

1. Discuss and view visuals of clothing designs, particularly suit coats and neckties.
2. With black marker, draw a large U at the top of the paper to represent the bottom of a person's face. Add a neck and shoulders.
3. Draw the lines of suit coat lapels, a shirt collar, and a necktie.
4. Add the lines of patterns and designs to the necktie.
5. Add lines for the texture of the hair.
6. Draw the bottom of a nose, a mouth, and chin on the face.
7. Color in everything except the necktie with crayons.
8. Color in the necktie with colored markers.

Questions for Discussion

Why would a clothing designer be a type of artist? What type of patterns or designs did you create? How did you create texture for the hair? Can you tell how the person is feeling?

Share Time/Evaluation

_____
_____
_____
_____

Curriculum Connection

Social Studies, Language Arts

Smiley Face

Objectives/Concepts

1. To experiment with painting technique.
2. To experiment with printing technique.
3. To work with color, shape, and texture.
4. To experience color mixing.
5. To create a pattern.

Technique

Painting, Cutting and Pasting, Printing

Materials

12 in. x 18 in. white paper
Tempera paints (primary colors, white, black)
Brushes
Sponges cut in 1-in. pieces
4 in. x 6 in. red paper
Glue
Scissors

Alternate Materials

Construction paper, crayons (wax or oil), yarn, watercolor paints, colored chalk, pastels

Activities/Process

1. Discuss and view visuals of faces and facial features. Smiles and dental health can be explored.
2. Paint a large oval for the face and neck, mixing red, yellow, and white. Blue can be added to make brown hues.
3. Paint the facial features except for the mouth.
4. Paint the hair.
5. Paint the clothing on the shoulders in a pattern.
6. Cut the red paper to make a mouth.
7. Glue down.
8. Use white paint on sponge to print teeth on red mouth.

Questions for Discussion

What colors did you use to make the face? How did you make the texture for the hair? What is printing? What kind of expression does your person have? What type of pattern is in the clothing? How did you make some of your colors?

Share Time/Evaluation

_____

_____

_____

Curriculum Connection

Science, Social Studies, Language Arts

Electric Body Design

Objectives/Concepts

1. To use line, shape, and color.
2. To use repetition.
3. To vary sizes of lines and shapes.
4. To stylize body forms into stick figures.
5. To experiment with a variety of body positions.
6. To create rhythm and movement.
7. To work with negative space.

Technique

Drawing

Materials

12 in. x 18 in. white drawing paper
Black marker
Colored markers

Alternate Materials

Crayons (wax or oil), colored pencils

Activities/Process

1. Discuss body movement.
2. Using student models, position bodies into various positions.
3. Demonstrate drawing stick figures of the body form. Use ovals for the head, hands, and feet, and lines for the body, arms, and legs.
4. Change the position of the bodies and make some larger and some smaller.
5. Outline around the bodies with colored markers. Continue outlining until all the negative space has been filled in. Stop when you reach another line.

Questions for Discussion

Where are there joints in our bodies? How do our bodies move? What makes the drawing look like it has movement? Would you be able to put your body in the same positions as the figures in your drawing?

Share Time/Evaluation

_____
_____
_____
_____

Curriculum Connection

Science, Music

Looking Out the Window

Objectives/Concepts

1. To work with line, shape, and color.
2. To work with facial features.
3. To work with proportion.
4. To create expression.
5. To create texture.
6. To create patterns.
7. To experiment with drawing technique.
8. To experiment with painting technique.
9. To create an impression of transparency.

Technique

Drawing, Painting

Materials

11 in. x 17 in. white paper
12 in. x 18 in. black paper
Black crayon
Watercolor paints

½ in. x 18 in. black strips
  (2 per child)
½ in. x 12 in. black strips
  (3 per child)
Glue

Alternate Materials

Colored crayons, colored chalk, tempera paints

Activities/Process

1. Discuss and view visuals of faces and hands. If a large mirror is available, have students place their hands on the mirror and look at themselves.
2. With black crayon, trace both hands palms down on the bottom part of the paper.
3. Draw a large oval for a head.
4. Add neck and shoulders. Patterns can be added to the clothing.
5. Draw facial features and hair.
6. Paint in with watercolors.
7. Glue the two long black strips over the picture, lengthwise and equally spaced. Glue the three shorter black strips sideways to resemble a window pane. Glue or staple to black paper.

Questions for Discussion

What does transparent mean? What does proportion mean? How does it look like your person is feeling? What patterns did you make? How did you create the texture for the hair? What happened when you painted over the crayon lines?

Share Time/Evaluation

_____

_____

_____

Curriculum Connection

Science, Language Arts, Math

Stick Puppets

Objectives/Concepts

1. To work with line, shape, and color.
2. To create texture.
3. To create pattern.
4. To experiment with three dimensions.
5. To experiment with cutting and pasting technique.
6. To experiment with drawing technique.

Technique

Drawing, Cutting and Pasting

Materials

6 in. x 9 in. oak tag (2 per child)
Pencil
Colored markers (fine-line)
Craft stick
Glue
Scissors

Alternate Materials

Variety of colored paper, yarn, felt, fabric, crayons

Activities/Process

1. Discuss the characters in a story, poem, or song.
2. Draw a large person or character on the oak tag. Make sure the parts are thick enough to cut out.
3. Layer the two pieces of oak tag together and cut out the person.
4. Decorate one piece with colored markers as the front view.
5. Decorate the other piece as the back view.
6. Glue the craft stick to the back of one figure.
7. Glue the second piece to fit the first piece, sandwiching the craft stick between the two pieces of oak tag.

Questions for Discussion

What is a puppet? Why is it fun to make puppets? What does three-dimensional mean? Did you use a pattern on the clothing? What other details did you make? What did you do to make texture in the hair? Did you have a particular person or character in mind before you made your puppet? What did you need to think about to make the puppet look like that person or character?

Share Time/Evaluation

_____

_____

_____

_____

Curriculum Connection

Science, Social Studies, Language Arts

Paper Bag Puppet

Objectives/Concepts

1. To work with three dimensions.
2. To create texture.
3. To work with facial features.
4. To create emotion.
5. To experiment with cutting and pasting technique.

Technique

Sculpture, Cutting and Pasting

Materials

Lunch-size paper bag
Scraps of colored paper
Newspaper
Scissors
Glue
Tape or string

Alternate Materials

Variety of papers, yarn, buttons, felt, ribbon

Activities/Process

1. Discuss visual characteristics of faces of family members, storybook characters, neighborhood helpers, or other people.
2. Stuff paper bag with newspaper.
3. Tape or tie a string around the neck area.
4. With construction paper, cut and paste the facial features.
5. Add the hair.

Questions for Discussion

What is a puppet? Who is your puppet? Why did you have to put hair on the back of the paper bag? How is your puppet feeling at this time? Could you tell us something about your puppet?

Share Time/Evaluation

_____
_____
_____
_____

Curriculum Connection

Science, Social Studies, Language Arts

Colorful Bird

Objectives/Concepts

1. To work with color, shape, and line.
2. To work with positive and negative shape.
3. To work with contour.
4. To experiment with drawing technique.

Technique

Drawing

Materials

12 in. x 18 in. white paper
Oil crayons

Alternate Materials

Colored chalk, tempera paints, watercolor
paints

Activities/Process

1. Discuss and show visuals on birds.
2. Draw a large colorful bird that fills most of the paper. Outline the parts with black.
3. In the negative spaces that are left, follow the contours of the bird outline and the edge of the paper and make colorful shapes. Outline the shapes with black.

Questions for Discussion

What shapes can we use to make a bird? What is the difference between a positive shape and a negative shape? What does outlining the bird and the shapes do for the picture? What is contour? Did you blend any colors?

Share Time/Evaluation

_____
_____
_____
_____

Curriculum Connection

Science, Social Studies

Baby Owls

Objectives/Concepts

1. To work with shape and color.
2. To create texture.
3. To experience cutting and pasting technique.
4. To experience printing technique.
5. To explore paper tearing.

Technique

Printing, Cutting and Pasting

Materials

12 in. x 18 in. blue paper
Tempera paint (white, brown, and yellow)
Sponges in 1-in. pieces
6 in. x 12 in. brown paper
Green, yellow, and brown paper scraps

Alternate Materials

Colored chalk, pastels

Activities/Process

1. Discuss and view visuals about baby owls.
2. Using a sponge and white paint, print two or three oval shapes side by side.
3. With brown paint, print a few times over the white.
4. With yellow paint, print a few times over the brown and white.
5. Cut a tree limb from the brown paper, using rectangle shapes.
6. Add green leaves by tearing small pieces of paper and gluing them on top of each other.
7. From black scraps, cut and glue down eyes.
8. From yellow scraps, cut and glue down feet and beaks.

Questions for Discussion

What would a baby owl feel like if you could touch it? What is the difference between painting and printing? How does tearing the green paper make it seem more like the texture of leaves? How are your baby owls alike? How are they different?

Share Time/Evaluation

_____
_____
_____
_____

Curriculum Connection

Science, Social Studies

Patterned Bird

Objectives/Concepts

1. To work with the elements of line.
2. To work with shape and color.
3. To create patterns.

Technique

Drawing

Materials

12 in. x 18 in. drawing paper
Colored markers

Alternate Materials

Crayons (wax or oil), colored pencils

Activities/Process

1. Discuss and view visuals of birds (fish, insects or other subjects could be used as well).
2. With black marker, make a large bird that fills the page.
3. Divide the inside of the bird with black lines.
4. Fill in these areas with different patterns, using colored markers.

Questions for Discussion

What are some different lines and where did you use them? What kind of patterns did you use? Which is your favorite pattern?

Share Time/Evaluation

_____
_____
_____
_____

Curriculum Connection

Science, Social Studies, Language Arts, Math

Feathered Friends

Objectives/Concepts

1. To work with color, shape, and size.
2. To experiment with cutting and pasting.
3. To experiment with contour line.
4. To experiment with painting technique.
5. To work with primary colors.

Technique

Cutting and Pasting, Painting

Materials

12 in. x 18 in. white or manila paper
6 in. x 9 in. construction paper in various
   colors
Scissors
Glue
Tempera paint (red, yellow, and blue)
Brushes

Alternate Materials

Crayons (wax or oil), variety of papers, feathers, chalk, pastels

Activities/Process

1. Discuss and show visuals of birds.
2. With construction paper, cut an oval for the bird's body, a circle for the head, and triangles for the tail and wings. Glue to the large paper. Add eye and beak.
3. Using one of the primary colors, paint a thick line around the contour (outline) of the bird.
4. Using a second primary color, paint around the first line following the contour.
5. Using the last primary color, paint in the rest of the paper.

Questions for Discussion

What are some of the body parts of a bird? What kind of shape did you use to make the bird? What are the three primary colors? Why are they important? What is the contour edge?

Share Time/Evaluation

_____
_____
_____

_____

Curriculum Connection

Science, Social Studies

Clay Bird in Nest

Objectives/Concepts

1. To work in three dimensions.
2. To experiment with clay technique.
3. To create texture.

Technique

Sculpture

Materials

Clay (plasticine or self-hardening,
   about the size of a tennis ball)
Feathers
Small buttons or craft eyes
Toothpick or craft stick

Activities/Process

1. Discuss and show visuals of birds and nests.
2. Demonstrate how to mold clay by pinching, pulling, and joining.
3. Break clay in half.
4. With one half of clay, make a ball. Make a pinch pot by sticking thumb into the clay and pinching while turning the clay around.
5. With the other half of the clay make a bird. Break a piece off for the head and roll it into a ball. Roll the other piece for the body and attach it to the head by smoothing the clay together.
6. Push in the buttons for the eyes and pinch out a beak.
7. Add a feather for the tail and one for each wing.
8. With a craft stick or toothpick, make lines in the nest and bird to create texture.

Questions for Discussion

Where does clay come from? How does it feel? What does three-dimensional mean? What do you have to do to make sure the separate clay pieces will not fall apart? How would a bird feel if you held one carefully?

Share Time/Evaluation

_____
_____
_____
_____

Curriculum Connection

Science, Social Studies

Tropical Bird Mobile

Objectives/Concepts

1. To work with line, shape, and color.
2. To create texture.
3. To work with layering.
4. To experiment with three dimensions.
5. To experiment with sculpture.
6. To create a mobile.

Technique

Sculpture, Cutting and Pasting

Materials

9 in. x 12 in. colored paper
   (5 per child; 2 pieces
   should be the same color)

Assorted colored paper scraps	Glue
Scissors	Paper punch
Colored markers	String

Alternate Materials

Feathers, variety of papers, buttons, craft eyes, glitter

Activities/Process

1. Discuss and show visuals of tropical birds.
2. Fold one piece of paper in half. Cut a half circle from one end to the other for the body of the bird. Do not cut off the fold.
3. Fold another paper in half and cut a complete circle shape. Glue the two circles together on each side of the folded half-circle for the head.
4. Hold 2 pieces of the same color paper together to cut the wings. Cut feather shapes out of colored paper and glue them to the wings. Glue the wings to the body.
5. Cut the tail from the last piece of paper. Add colored paper feathers to the tail and glue the tail to the body.
6. Add eyes and a beak.
7. Punch a hole in the middle of the back and attach string for hanging.

Questions for Discussion

What are the parts of a bird? What is a tropical bird? How did you show texture on your bird? How did you make both wings the same? Where did you use layering? What is a mobile? Why is your bird considered three-dimensional?

Share Time/Evaluation

_____
_____
_____

Curriculum Connection

Science, Social Studies

Tall Birds

Objectives/Concepts

1. To experiment with watercolor technique.
2. To experiment with primary and secondary colors.
3. To work with texture.
4. To mix colors.

Technique

Painting

Materials

12 in. x 18 in. white paper
Watercolor paints
Black fine-line marker

Alternate Materials

Tempera paints, chalk, pastels, crayons (wax or oil),
construction paper, feathers

Activities/Process

1. Discuss and view visuals of birds.
2. Choose a secondary color. With watercolor paints, use that secondary color, and the two primary colors that make that color, to paint a body, head, tail, wings, long thin legs, beak, and eye.
3. Use both wet and dry brush techniques.
4. When dry, outline with black marker.

Questions for Discussion

What are the main parts of a bird? Name the primary colors. What color did you get when you mixed two colors together? Why are there differences in the secondary color you mixed?

Share Time/Evaluation

_____

_____

_____

_____

Curriculum Connection

Science, Social Studies

Animal Mosaics

Objectives/Concepts

1. To work with shape and color.
2. To create texture.
3. To experience mosaic art.
4. To experiment with cutting and pasting technique.
5. To work with silhouette.

Technique

Cutting and Pasting

Materials

12 in. x 18 in. colored paper
12 in. x 18 in. black paper
1 in. strips of assorted colored paper
Scissors
Glue
Pencil

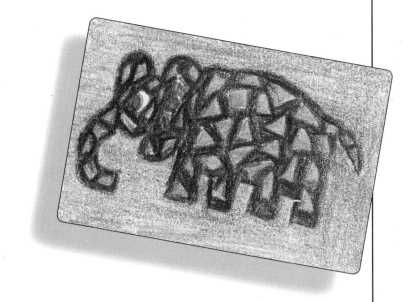

Alternate Materials

Various papers, seeds, beans

Activities/Process

1. Discuss and view visuals of animals.
2. Discuss and view visuals about the art of mosaic.
3. On the black paper, draw a silhouette of an animal large enough to fill the whole page. Make the body parts, such as the legs and tail, thick. Cut out the animal.
4. With 1-inch strips, cut triangles of a chosen color. Arrange and glue the triangles on top of the black animal, close together but leaving a little black showing between the triangles. The mosaic triangles can be all the same color or multiple colors.
5. Glue the mosaic animal to the large piece of colored paper.

Questions for Discussion

What is mosaic art? What was used for the materials long ago? Why was it important to make your animal with thick body parts? Was there a reason behind your color choices? What did you do to make the pieces fit into the silhouette shape of your animal?

Share Time/Evaluation

_____
_____
_____
_____

Curriculum Connection

Science, Social Studies, Math

Zebra Skins

Objectives/Concepts

1. To work with line.
2. To create pattern.
3. To create texture.
4. To experiment with the idea of camouflage.

Technique

Painting

Materials

12 in. x 18 in. white or black paper
Black or white tempera paint

Alternate Materials

Chalk, charcoal, construction paper

Activities/Process

1. Discuss and view visuals of zebras.
2. Choose either black paint on white paper or white paint on black paper.
3. Paint lines to represent the texture of zebra skin filling the paper.

Questions for Discussion

What does a zebra look like? Are the patterns on all zebras the same? Why do you think animals have patterns on their bodies? Where would you find zebras and how does the pattern on their coats help them?

Share Time/Evaluation

_____
_____
_____
_____

Curriculum Connection

Science, Social Studies

Snakes

Objectives/Concepts

1. To work with line and color.
2. To create a twist or coil.
3. To create a pattern.

Technique

Drawing

Materials

12 in. x 18 in. drawing paper
12 in. x 18 in. colored paper
Colored markers
Scissors
Glue

Alternate Materials

Crayons (wax or oil), colored pencils, watercolor paints, tempera paints

Activities/Process

1. Discuss and view pictures of snakes.
2. Talk about patterns.
3. Draw a large snake with a twist or coil in its body. Make sure the body is thick enough to design and cut.
4. Design the snake with a pattern.
5. Cut snake out and glue down onto colored paper.

Questions for Discussion

How does a snake move? What kind of pattern did you use? Where do you think we would find your snake? Would it be spotted easily or would it be camouflaged?

Share Time/Evaluation

_____
_____
_____
_____

Curriculum Connection

Science, Social Studies, Math

Giraffes

Objectives/Concepts

1. To work with shape and color.
2. To work with primary colors.
3. To experience tempera painting technique.
4. To work with pattern.
5. To work with overlapping.

Technique

Painting

Materials

12 in. x 18 in. white paper
Tempera paints (red, yellow, blue, and black)

Alternate Materials

Watercolor paints, crayons (wax or oil), construction paper

Activities/Process

1. Discuss and view visuals of giraffes.
2. Discuss primary colors.
3. Discuss the body shape of a giraffe.
4. Paint the body, neck, head, and legs of one giraffe yellow.
5. Paint a second giraffe behind the first, so that the first giraffe overlaps the second one.
6. Paint in the spaces around the giraffes with red and blue.
7. Paint black spots on the giraffes.
8. Add eyes and mouth.

Questions for Discussion

What can you tell me about a giraffe? What are primary colors and why are they important? Where did you overlap? Which giraffe is in front of the other one? Are all the spots on a giraffe the same?

Share Time/Evaluation

_____
_____
_____
_____

Curriculum Connection

Science, Social Studies, Math

Giraffe

Objectives/Concepts
1. To work with shape and color.
2. To create texture.
3. To experiment with cutting and pasting techniques.
4. To experiment with printing techniques.

Technique
Cutting and Pasting, Printing

Materials
9 in. x 12 in. yellow paper
6 in. x 9 in. yellow paper
4½ in. x 12 in. yellow paper
3 in. x 12 in. yellow paper (4 per child)
3 in. x 3 in. black paper (4 per child)
Black scraps
Scissors
Glue
1 in. sponge pieces
Brown paint

Alternate Materials
Crayons, tempera paint, markers

Activities/Process
1. Discuss and view visuals of giraffes.
2. Round the edges of the large rectangle for the body.
3. Round the edges of the smaller rectangle for the head.
4. Glue the head to one end and the body to the other of the long fat rectangle, which becomes the neck.
5. Glue the long, thinner rectangles on as legs.
6. Add eye and mouth with scrap black paper.
7. Add black squares as hooves.
8. Dip sponge into brown paint and print spots all over the giraffe's body.

Questions for Discussion
Why do you think giraffes have long necks? Why might they have spots on their coats? How did we change a rectangle into an oval? What can you tell me about printing?

Share Time/Evaluation
_____
_____
_____

Curriculum Connection
Science, Social Studies, Math

Penguins

Objectives/Concepts
1. To work with color and shape.
2. To experiment with painting technique.
3. To work with different viewpoints.

Technique
Painting

Materials
12 in. x 18 in. blue paper
Tempera paint (black, white, yellow)
Brushes (one large, one small)

Alternate Materials
Oil crayons, construction paper

Activities/Process
1. Discuss and view visuals about penguins.
2. With the large brush, paint several black bodies of penguins in different sizes on different parts of the paper. Use a larger circle on the bottom and a smaller circle on the top, like the shape of a number 8 or a bowling pin.
3. Add little wings to both sides of the body if the penguin is going to be facing front or back. Paint only one wing if the penguin is side view.
4. With the small brush, paint white bellies in the middle of the black for a front view, and on one side for a side view.
5. Paint either two white eyes, one, or none depending on which way the penguin is facing. Add a black spot for the center of the eye.
6. Add yellow feet and beaks.

Questions for Discussion
Where do we find penguins? What have we learned about penguins? Which way are your penguins facing? What happened if the bottom layer of paint was not completely dry when you put another color over it?

Share Time/Evaluation
_____
_____
_____
_____

Curriculum Connection
Science, Social Studies, Math

Spider and Web

Objectives/Concepts

1. To work with circles of varying sizes.
2. To work with line.
3. To experiment with watercolor techniques.
4. To experience color mixing.

Technique

Drawing, Painting

Materials

12 in. x 18 in. white drawing paper
Black crayon
Watercolor paints

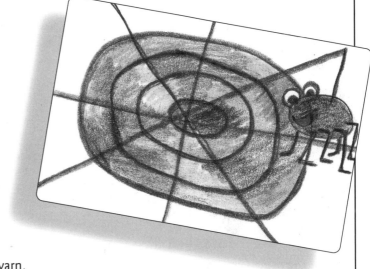

Alternate Materials

Tempera paints, crayons (oil or wax), string or yarn,
construction paper, scissors, glue

Activities/Process

1. Discuss spiders and their webs.
2. Make a small circle in the middle of the paper.
3. Make a larger circle around the first, then a larger one around that one. Keep adding bigger circles until they almost reach the edge of the paper.
4. Divide the circle with straight lines from the middle of the paper outward.
5. Draw a line down from one line, and a spider hanging from it. Make the spider large and fill in with black crayon.
6. Paint the spider's web with watercolors.

Questions for Discussion

Have you ever seen a spider's web? Where? Why do spiders make webs? What happened to the paint colors when they touched each other?

Share Time/Evaluation

_____

_____

_____

_____

Curriculum Connection

Science, Social Studies, Language Arts, Math

Painted Turtles

Objectives/Concepts

1. To experiment with watercolor technique.
2. To work with line, shape, and color.
3. To create a texture.
4. To experiment with color mixing.

Technique

Drawing, Painting

Materials

12 in. x 18 in. white paper
Watercolor paints
Black crayon

Alternate Materials

Tempera paints, crayons (oil or wax), colored chalk, pastels

Activities/Process

1. Discuss and view visuals of turtles.
2. Discuss shape and texture.
3. Demonstrate making a large half-circle for the turtle's body with black crayon.
4. Add head, legs, and tail.
5. Make squares on the shell to represent texture.
6. Paint with watercolors.
7. Add environment around the turtle.

Questions for Discussion

Where do turtles live? How do their shells feel? What happened when two colors of paints were close to each other? Did you mix any colors? What did you do to make it look like the shell was bumpy?

Share Time/Evaluation

_____

_____

_____

_____

Curriculum Connection

Science, Social Studies, Math

Torn-Paper Animals

Objectives/Concepts

1. To work with line, shape, and color.
2. To create texture.
3. To experiment with tearing.
4. To work with layering.
5. To work with overlapping.
6. To experiment with cutting and pasting technique.

Technique

Cutting and Pasting

Materials

9 in. x 12 in. colored paper (animal fur colors)
Assorted colored scrap paper
Scissors
Glue

Alternate Materials

Craft eyes, buttons, yarn

Activities/Process

1. Discuss and view visuals of animals.
2. Choose a colored paper for an animal and carefully tear the shape of an oval for the body.
3. Tear another sheet of the same color for the head and glue it to the body.
4. Tear four rectangles for the legs and glue to the body.
5. Tear the shape of the tail and add to the body.
6. With the leftover scraps, tear small pieces and glue them onto the body, layering and overlapping them to create the texture of fur.
7. Cut out eyes, nose, mouth, ears, and whiskers and glue down.

Questions for Discussion

What shapes are animal's bodies? What shapes are their heads? What shapes are their tails? What shapes are their legs? How would it feel to pat a real animal? How do you think the animal you made would feel? Was it difficult to tear the shape you wanted to make? Why? Did it need to be a perfect shape?

Share Time/Evaluation

_____

_____

_____

_____

Curriculum Connection

Science, Social Studies

Clay Animals

Objectives/Concepts
1. To work with shape.
2. To experiment with three dimensions.
3. To create texture.
4. To experiment with clay.

Technique
Sculpture

Materials
Self-hardening clay
Pointed craft stick

Alternate Materials
Plasticine clay, papier-mâché, plastic knife
and fork

Activities/Process
1. Discuss and view visuals of animals.
2. Break clay in two pieces. Make one piece twice the size of the other.
3. Roll the large piece of clay into a thick potato shape.
4. With pointed craft stick make lines down the clay, lengthwise and sideways, resembling a plus sign.
5. Pull thick legs from each of the four sections. Make legs short and fat in order to hold the weight of the clay body.
6. Roll the small piece of clay for the head and smooth it onto the body so it becomes one piece of clay.
7. Pinch clay to make ears, nose, and tail.
8. Use the pointed craft stick or a pencil to make eyes and textures.

Questions for Discussion
How does the clay feel? Why should you avoid adding small, delicate parts to your clay sculpture? Why do you think we pinched the legs from the body instead of attaching them? Why is it important to smooth the clay from one piece to the other? Why do we call sculpture three-dimensional? How did you show texture on your clay?

Share Time/Evaluation
_____
_____
_____
_____

Curriculum Connection
Science, Social Studies

Tooth Person Brushing Hair

Objectives/Concepts

1. To work with line, shape, and color.
2. To work with layering.
3. To create pattern.
4. To create texture.
5. To work with facial features and expression.
6. To experiment with cutting and pasting technique.

Technique

Cutting and Pasting

Materials

9 in. x 12 in. white paper, cut in the shape of a tooth
Assorted construction paper scraps
1 in. x 9 in. strip of colored paper
3 in. x 2 in. white paper
Scissors
Glue

Alternate Materials

Variety of papers, yarn, fabric, felt, ribbon, buttons

Activities/Process

1. Discuss and show visuals about teeth and tooth care.
2. Using the tooth-shaped paper, add details of facial features.
3. Curl, fringe, and cut paper to make hair.
4. Add clothing with bows, buttons, and patterns.
5. Shoes can be added to the bottoms for feet.
6. Make a toothbrush by gluing the small white paper to the colored paper strip. Fringe the white paper to look like a brush.
7. Glue the toothbrush to one arm in the position of brushing the top of the tooth's head.

Questions for Discussion

Describe the different shapes and sizes of our teeth. What functions do various teeth have? How should we take care of our teeth? What does brushing teeth do? What kind of patterns did you make? What type of expression does the face on your tooth have? How did you fringe the paper? How did you make the texture of the tooth's hair?

Share Time/Evaluation

_____
_____
_____

Curriculum Connection

Science

Tooth Fairy

Objectives/Concepts

1. To work with line and shape.
2. To experiment with color mixing.
3. To experiment with drawing technique.
4. To experiment with painting technique.

Technique

Drawing, Painting

Materials

12 in. x 18 in. white paper
Black crayon
Watercolor paints

Alternate Materials

Tempera paint, crayons (wax or oil), colored chalk

Activities/Process

1. Discuss the importance of dental health.
2. Imagine what a tooth fairy might look like.
3. Draw a large tooth fairy with black crayon.
4. Paint in with watercolors.

Questions for Discussion

What do we use teeth for? Why is it important to keep our teeth healthy? Why do we lose teeth? Do you do anything when you lose a tooth? Has anyone seen a tooth fairy? What do you think a tooth fairy looks like? Do you think there might be more than one? What happened when you mixed colors together? What colors did you make?

Share Time/Evaluation

_____
_____
_____
_____

Curriculum Connection

Science

Flying Tooth Fairy

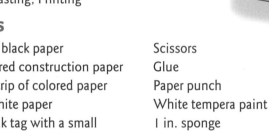

Objectives/Concepts

1. To work with line, shape, and color.
2. To create texture.
3. To create pattern.
4. To work with repetition.
5. To work with positive and negative shapes.
6. To experiment with cutting and pasting technique.
7. To experiment with printing technique.

Technique

Cutting and Pasting, Printing

Materials

12 in. x 18 in. black paper	Scissors
Assorted colored construction paper	Glue
½ in. x 9 in. strip of colored paper	Paper punch
1 in. x 3 in. white paper	White tempera paint
2 in. x 2 in. oak tag with a small tooth shape cut out of it	1 in. sponge

Alternate Materials

Crayons (wax or oil), colored chalk, colored markers, tempera paint, watercolor paint

Activities/Process

1. Discuss and view visuals about dental health.
2. Discuss imagination and what we think a tooth fairy might look like if we saw one.
3. Make a toothbrush by gluing the small white paper to the strip of colored paper. Cut fringe on the white paper to look like a brush.
4. Using colored paper cut out the head, body, arms, and legs of a tooth fairy. The body, arms, and legs can be cut and glued to appear in side view. Arrange and glue so that the tooth fairy will be sitting on the toothbrush.
5. Add clothing, hair, hats, shoes, and other details.
6. Glue the tooth fairy and the toothbrush to the middle of the black paper.
7. Punch out some white dots for the stars. Glue down.
8. Place the tooth-shaped stencil on the black paper. Make a print by dipping the sponge in white paint and pressing over the tooth-shaped space. Repeat this several times around the paper.

Questions for Discussion

Why is it important to take care of our teeth? What is a stencil? What is printing? What happened if you put too much paint on the sponge or pressed too hard? What did you have to do to make it look like the tooth fairy was riding the toothbrush?

Share Time/Evaluation

_____

_____

_____

Curriculum Connection

Science

Painted Tree on Newspaper

Objectives/Concepts

1. To realize trees are used to make paper.
2. To work with shape, line, and color.
3. To work with various thicknesses.
4. To experience color mixing.
5. To experiment with painting technique.
6. To experiment with texture.

Technique

Painting

Materials

Newspaper cut into 11 in. x 13½ in. sheets (half of a half sheet)
12 in. x 18 in. brown paper
Tempera paint (brown, black, green, blue, and yellow)

Alternate Materials

Watercolor paints, construction paper (brown, shades of green), crayons (wax or oil), colored chalk, pastels, charcoal

Activities/Process

1. Discuss the paper-making process and where paper comes from.
2. Discuss and view visuals of trees. Talk about the parts of a tree and the change in thickness from trunk to branch to limb to twig.
3. Glue or staple the newspaper to the brown paper for matting.
4. With the paper held vertically, paint a large brown tree that fills the entire piece of paper. Add black lines for texture.
5. With green paint dab the leaves at the ends. Mix blue and yellow paint to make different shades of green.

Questions for Discussion

How is paper made? What else can we use trees for? How does a tree feel? What did you do to show the texture of the rough bark? How did you make different shades of green? What happened when you dabbed the paint?

Share Time/Evaluation

_____

_____

_____

_____

Curriculum Connection

Science, Social Studies, Language Arts

Newspaper Masks

Objectives/Concepts

1. To use newspaper as a paper medium.
2. To work with line, shape, and color.
3. To work with facial features.
4. To experiment with mask making.
5. To experiment with cutting and pasting technique.
6. To experiment with layering and overlapping.
7. To work with curling and fringing to create texture.
8. To work with symmetry.

Technique

Cutting and Pasting

Materials

12 in. x 18 in. colored construction paper
11 in. x 13½ in. newspaper (half of a half sheet)
Assorted construction paper scraps
Scissors
Glue

Alternate Materials

Tempera paints, crayons (wax or oil), markers, various papers, glitter, yarn, felt, beads, buttons

Activities/Process

1. Discuss and view visuals about masks.
2. Discuss facial features and expression.
3. Fold the piece of newspaper in half and cut the outside edge to make a mask shape.
4. Open the folded mask and glue it to the colored paper.
5. Using construction paper scraps, add facial features and details.
6. Add hair by curling, fringing, or crimping.

Questions for Discussion

What are masks and what are they used for? What can be done to show emphasis on a certain part of the mask? How did you make both sides of the mask the same? What did you have to do to make both eyes or ears the same? What could your mask represent or be used for?

Share Time/Evaluation

_____
_____
_____
_____

Curriculum Connection

Science, Social Studies, Language Arts

Person Reading

Objectives/Concepts

1. To work with line, shape, and color.
2. To work with layering and overlapping.
3. To work with texture through curling and fringing.
4. To work with facial features and proportion.
5. To experiment with cutting and pasting.

Technique

Cutting and Pasting

Materials

9 in. x 12 in. salmon, pink, eggshell, tan, or brown paper
6 in. x 9 in. salmon, pink, eggshell, tan, or brown paper
Construction paper scraps in assorted colors
9 in. x 12 in. colored paper or newspaper
Scissors
Glue

Alternate Materials

Various papers, yarn, buttons, felt, fabric scraps, crayons
(wax or oil), markers

Activities/Process

1. Discuss importance of reading.
2. Discuss and view visuals of heads and facial features.
3. Round the edges of the large salmon, pink, eggshell, tan, or brown paper to make an oval for the face.
4. Add facial features and hair.
5. Trace hands on smaller salmon, pink, eggshell, tan, or brown paper and cut out (these can be premade for younger children).
6. If using newspaper, fold the piece of newspaper and glue the hands on so that the person appears to be reading it. If using colored paper, fold the paper and make it into a book cover by using scraps of paper, crayons, or markers. Add the hands to hold the book.
7. Glue the newspaper or the book below the head so that the person appears to be reading it.

Questions for Discussion

Why is reading important? What is your favorite book? What is your person reading in the newspaper? Where did you place the facial features in order to have the correct proportion? How did you make the eyes and ears the same?

Share Time/Evaluation

_____

_____

_____

Curriculum Connection

Science, Social Studies, Language Arts

Turkey

Objectives/Concepts

1. To work with line, shape, and color.
2. To create pattern.
3. To create texture.
4. To experiment with drawing technique.
5. To experiment with cutting and pasting technique.
6. To experiment with printing technique.

Technique

Drawing, Cutting and Pasting, Printing

Materials

Scissors
9 in. white paper circle
2 in. x 12 in. red paper strip
1 in. x 1 in. black paper (2 per child)
1½ in. x 1½ in. white paper
   (2 per child)

3 in. x 9 in. colored
   rectangles shaped like
   feathers (5 per child)
1 in. x 1 in. yellow paper
2 in. x 2 in. yellow paper
   (2 per child)

1 in. x 2 in. corrugated
   cardboard
Colored markers
Glue
Black tempera paint

Alternate Materials

Crayons (wax or oil), feathers, craft eyes

Activities/Process

1. Discuss and view visuals of turkeys.
2. With colored markers, create patterns and designs on the 9-inch circle. Although young children will not comprehend the word "radial," have students start from the center and make their design outward around the circle. For older children radial designs can be discussed in more detail.
3. Make a loop with the red strip and glue it to the bottom of the circle to create the neck and head.
4. Round both white squares together to make circles for the eyes.
5. Round both black squares together and glue on top of the white rounds.
6. Fold the yellow squares to make triangles. Glue the small one on for the beak. Glue the two larger ones to the bottom of the circle for the feet.
7. Paint the edge of the corrugated cardboard and print lines on the feathers for texture.
8. Glue the feathers to the back of the circle so that they show above the circle when viewed from the front.

Questions for Discussion

Why do we have Thanksgiving feasts with turkeys? How did you make texture on the feathers? What type of patterns did you make? Do you have a favorite pattern? How did you change a square into a circle? Why did we cut two pieces of paper at the same time?

Share Time/Evaluation

_____
_____
_____

Curriculum Connection

Science, Social Studies, Math

Woven Scarecrows

Objectives/Concepts

1. To work with color, line, and shape.
2. To create texture.
3. To experience weaving.
4. To create pattern.
5. To work with fringing.
6. To experiment with cutting and pasting.

Technique

Cutting and Pasting

Materials

$4\frac{1}{2}$ in. x 6 in. colored paper (2 per child)
$\frac{1}{4}$ in. x 6 in. strips of paper
Assorted construction paper scraps
$\frac{1}{4}$ in. x 9 in. brown paper strip
Scissors
Glue

Alternate Materials

Colored markers, scraps of material, dried hay, buttons

Activities/Process

1. Discuss and view visuals of scarecrows.
2. In the middle of one $4\frac{1}{2}$ x 6 paper, cut several slits about $\frac{1}{4}$ inch apart. Leave $\frac{1}{4}$ inch uncut border around all edges.
3. Weave the $\frac{1}{4}$ x 6 strips through the slits in an under-and-over pattern, alternating every other row.
4. Add colored paper rectangles for arms.
5. With the other $4\frac{1}{2}$ x 6 paper, create pant legs by cutting away a triangle shape from one of the $4\frac{1}{2}$-inch sides. Glue to the shirt.
6. Pockets, belts, buttons, and patches can be added with colored paper.
7. Cut a circle or oval for the head and add facial features. Glue to the body.
8. Cut paper fringe to resemble hay and glue to the bottom of the sleeves, pants, and neck areas.
9. Glue the scarecrow to the brown paper strip.
10. A bird can be cut and glued onto the shoulder of the scarecrow.

Questions for Discussion

Why do we have scarecrows? What are scarecrows usually made of? What is weaving? How did you create texture?

Share Time/Evaluation

_____

_____

_____

Curriculum Connection

Social Studies, Science, Language Arts

E

Snowman in a Snowstorm

Objectives/Concepts

1. To experiment with printmaking techniques.
2. To work with line, shape, and color.
3. To create size differences.

Technique

Printing, Cutting and Pasting

Materials

11 in. x 14 in. dark blue paper
Large, shallow box (from case of soda cans)
White tempera paint
Small container
Plastic spoon
Marble
White paper squares in three sizes (2 in., 3 in., and 4 in.)
Colored construction paper scraps
Glue
Scissors

Alternate Materials

Crayons (wax or oil), markers, buttons, ribbon

Activities/Process

1. Discuss and view visuals of snowstorms and snowmen.
2. Using the spoon, dip the marble in white paint and roll it until it is covered.
3. Place paper in the box and drop the marble onto the paper.
4. Move the box from side to side to allow the marble to roll around the paper. The marble can be dipped in paint again if needed.
5. Using the three white squares, round the corners creating circles. Glue together to resemble snowman.
6. Add construction paper details—hat, scarf, face, etc.
7. Glue snowman onto paper.

Questions for Discussion

What do you notice in a snowstorm? How does the snow fall if it is windy? How can we make a circle from a square? Why is the smallest circle on top? Tell me something about your snowman. What kind of line did the marble make?

Share Time/Evaluation

_____

_____

_____

Curriculum Connection

Science, Social Studies, Math

Winter Scene

Objectives/Concepts

1. To work with multimedia.
2. To work with silhouette.
3. To experience drawing technique.
4. To experience cutting and pasting technique.
5. To experience printing technique.
6. To create foreground and background.
7. To experience color mixing.

Technique

Drawing, Cutting and Pasting, Printing

Materials

12 in. x 18 in. dark blue paper
Colored chalk
Black oil crayon
Assorted construction paper scraps   Scissors
2 in., 3 in., and 4 in. squares of white paper   White tempera paint
Glue   1 in. sponges

Alternate Materials

Cotton balls, various papers, buttons, fabric scraps

Activities/Process

1. Discuss and view visuals of winter scenes and snowmen.
2. Using colored chalk, blend colors to make a colorful sky.
3. Using black oil crayon, draw houses, mountains, trees, fences, etc. in the middle of the paper. Color in with black to create the silhouettes.
4. Cut circles from the three white squares and glue together to make a snowman.
5. With colored paper, add clothing and details.
6. Glue to the bottom of the paper in the foreground.
7. With sponge and white paint, print the snow on the ground.

Questions for Discussion

What is a silhouette? What makes something look like it is in the background? How did you show distance in your picture? What happened if you used a lot of paint on your sponge? What can you tell me about blending the colors of chalk?

Share Time/Evaluation

_____
_____
_____
_____

Curriculum Connection

Science, Social Studies

Paper Pottery

Objectives/Concepts

1. To work with shape.
2. To work with a variety of lines.
3. To create a pattern.
4. To experiment with drawing technique.
5. To experiment with cutting and pasting technique.

Technique

Cutting and Pasting, Drawing

Materials

12 in. x 18 in. brown paper
12 in. x 18 in. black paper
Black marker
Scissors
Glue

Alternate Materials

Black crayon (wax or oil), plasticine clay, self-hardening clay, brown and black tempera paint, brown watercolor paint

Activities/Process

1. Discuss and view visuals about clay pottery.
2. Fold the brown paper in half. Cut the unfolded edge to make the shape of a pot, vase, or urn.
3. Discuss different lines and patterns and decorate the pottery piece with black marker.
4. Glue pottery onto black paper.

Questions for Discussion

What is pottery? How can we use pottery? What materials are used to make pottery and where is it found? What types of lines did you use to decorate your pottery? How do you think clay pottery was designed? Why did we use brown and black for the colors of our pottery?

Share Time/Evaluation

_____
_____
_____
_____

Curriculum Connection

Science, Social Studies, Math, Language Arts

Dragons or Mythical Beasts

Objectives/Concepts

1. To explore folklore traditions of the dragon and mythical beasts.
2. To work with line, shape, and color.
3. To create texture.
4. To use imagination.

Technique

Drawing

Materials

12 in. x 18 in. white drawing paper
Black marker
Wax crayons

Alternate Materials

Colored pencils, black crayon, watercolor paints

Activities/Process

1. Discuss and view visuals of dragons and mythical beasts.
2. Note differences between European and Chinese dragons
   (evil versus respect).
3. Draw a simple body shape, large enough to fill the page. Make the body scaly.
4. Add a long pointed tail, feet with claws, and fire coming from nostrils and mouth.

Questions for Discussion

What can you tell me about a dragon? Do you know any stories about mythical beasts? What makes your dragon look dangerous or playful? How did you show texture?

Share Time/Evaluation

_____
_____
_____
_____

Curriculum Connection

Science, Social Studies, Language Arts

Positive and Negative Quilt

Objectives/Concepts

1. To work with line, shape, and color.
2. To work with positive and negative shapes.
3. To create a pattern.
4. To work with contour.
5. To work with symmetry.
6. To experiment with cutting and pasting technique.

Technique

Cutting and Pasting

Materials

12 in. x 12 in. white or colored paper,   Scissors
  divided into 3 in. squares   Glue
1½ in. x 3 in. colored papers,   Pencil
  (16 per child)

Alternate Materials

Variety of papers, oak tag stencils, chalk, sponges, tempera paint

Activities/Process

1. Discuss and show visuals about quilts.
2. Discuss positive and negative shapes.
3. Cut half of the shape of an object (tree, flower, apple, etc.) from one long side of one of the small papers. Make sure to leave a little of the paper on the top, the bottom, and the other side. Save both the negative and the positive pieces.
4. Use one piece to trace the half shape onto the other small papers. Make 16 pieces altogether.
5. Arrange the pieces in the squares. First glue the half rectangle with the negative space on one side of the 3-inch square. Then flip over the half shape that was cut out and fit it next to the negative shape, completing the shape.
6. All 16 squares will have this half-negative shape and half-positive shape. The colors chosen and the way the positive and negative shapes are arranged will determine the design of the overall quilt.

Questions for Discussion

What is a quilt? What is the difference between positive and negative shapes? Why is it important to choose an object that is symmetrical? What pattern did you use? Why did we need to use only the contour of the object and not a lot of detail?

Share Time/Evaluation

_____
_____
_____
_____

Curriculum Connection

Science, Social Studies, Math

Fraction Quilt

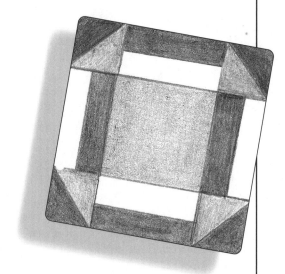

Objectives/Concepts

1. To work with horizontal, vertical, and diagonal straight lines.
2. To work with color.
3. To work with geometrical shapes.
4. To create pattern.
5. To experiment with drawing technique.

Technique

Drawing

Materials

12 in. x 12 in. white paper divided into 3-in. squares
Colored pencils
Ruler

Alternate Materials

Colored markers, crayons, colored paper cut into 3-in. squares

Activities/Process

1. Discuss and show visuals about quilts.
2. Make a pattern by dividing some squares with horizontal, vertical, or diagonal lines. Some squares can be left undivided. The entire paper should become one quilt square.
3. Color in.

Questions for Discussion

What is a quilt? How are parts put together to create the whole? What type of pattern did you use in your quilt square? How did you make your color choices? Some quilt patterns have names. Could you give your quilt square a name? Why would you name it that?

Share Time/Evaluation

_____
_____
_____
_____

Curriculum Connection

Science, Social Studies, Math, Language Arts

E

Textured Quilt

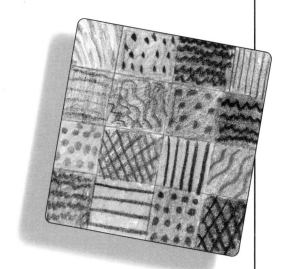

Objectives/Concepts

1. To work with line, shape, and color.
2. To create texture.
3. To work with pattern.
4. To experiment with crayon resist.
5. To experiment with crayon rubbing.
6. To experiment with printing technique.
7. To experiment with painting technique.

Technique

Printing, Painting

Materials

12 in. x 12 in. white paper, divided into 3-in. squares
Crayons (oil or wax)
Variety of textures (e.g., sandpaper, textured wallpaper, mesh netting, screening, corrugated cardboard)
Watercolor paints

Alternate Materials

Watered-down tempera paints

Activities/Process

1. Discuss and show visuals about quilts.
2. Discuss, show, and feel textures.
3. Place a texture under one of the white paper squares. Rub the flat part of a crayon over the entire square, exposing the texture that is underneath.
4. Choose different textures for different squares. The same texture can be used more than once.
5. When all the squares are filled in with textures, paint over each square using watercolors.

Questions for Discussion

What is a quilt? What is a texture? How do different textures feel? Can you find some textures around the room? Do any of the textures look like a pattern? Why did the crayon rubbing show a texture? What happened when you painted over the crayon rubbing?

Share Time/Evaluation

_____

_____

_____

_____

Curriculum Connection

Science, Social Studies, Math

Fireworks Celebration

Objectives/Concepts

1. To work with line, shape, and color.
2. To create blended colors.
3. To create movement.
4. To work with silhouette.
5. To create distance.
6. To work with overlapping.
7. To experiment with drawing technique.
8. To experiment with cutting and pasting technique.

Technique

Drawing, Cutting and Pasting

Materials

12 in. x 18 in. white paper
4 in. x 18 in. black paper
9 in. x 12 in. black paper
1½ in. x 2½ in. white paper

¼ in. x 6 in. black
    paper strip
Scissors
Colored chalk

Glue
Fine-line markers
    (blue and red)

Alternate Materials

Colored paper, stick-on stars, oil crayons

Activities/Process

1. Discuss fireworks and patriotic celebrations.
2. With colored chalk, make some lines on the top half of the paper that resemble bursting fireworks.
3. Glue the 4 x 18 black paper to the bottom of the large white paper.
4. With the 9 x 12 black paper, cut out the silhouette shapes of mountains, trees, houses, fences, or other landscape forms and glue above the 4 x 18 black paper, overlapping some of the fireworks.
5. On the small white paper, use the red and blue fine-line markers to make a symbol of the American flag. It is not necessary to make all the stripes and stars.
6. Cut the flag vertically (up and down) into thirds.
7. Glue down the black strip and glue the first third of the flag (the part with the blue square) onto the flag-pole.
8. Glue the middle part of the flag a little lower the first part.
9. Glue the last part of the flag a little higher than the middle part.

Questions for Discussion

Have you ever seen fireworks? When? What did they look like? How did you blend colors in your fireworks? What kinds of lines did you use? What is silhouette? How did you show distance? What makes the flag seem as if it is moving?

Share Time/Evaluation

_____
_____
_____

Curriculum Connection

Science, Social Studies, Language Arts

Conclusion

Art can foster learning in all areas of the curriculum. It can reinforce and enhance the learning of science, social studies, language arts, and math. Art provides a way to express in a visual form the world as we have observed it and reacted to it.

Through the process of self-expression, one needs to clarify the thought process, address the problem, and come up with a solution. Through art education, starting with the very young, children are able to train their observation skills and discriminate between shapes, colors, lines, and textures. Art strengthens the ability to notice detail.

Children are naturally curious and learn best through experience. Teachers and other adults can help children become sensitive to their world. The activities presented in this book should serve as a catalyst for many ways to use artistic media in the curriculum. Subject matters may be freely substituted to serve individual needs throughout the curriculum. The overall quality of the school's educational program is improved by the use of art in the classroom. Art experiences allow for individuality and encourage children to express themselves openly, which results in emotional, aesthetic, and conceptual growth.

Appendix A

The following materials are used throughout the various art lessons in this book. Additional materials may be used depending on individual creativity. The materials listed are safe for children, however adult supervision is always recommended when young children are working. Safety precautions should be utilized when children are cutting, stapling, or using sharp objects.

Aluminum foil	Markers	Paper clips
Beads	fine-line	Paper towels
Brayer	permanent	Pastels (chalk)
Brushes	round	Pen (ball point)
Buttons	washable	Pencil
Cardboard	Masking tape	Printing plate
Cellophane	Music	Ribbon
Chalk	Nature items	Ruler
Charcoal	Newspaper	Salt
Charcoal pencils	Oak tag	Sand
Clay (or plasticine)	Paint	Sandpaper
Colored pencils	acrylic	Scissors
Confetti	tempera	fancy-edged
Cotton swabs	watercolor	straight-edged
Craft eyes	Paintbrushes	Sponges
Crayons	Paper	Stapler
oil	bogus	Sticky dots
wax	brown wrapping	Straws
Fabric scraps	construction	String
Feathers	corrugated	Styrofoam
Foam board	crepe	packing
Glitter	gift wrapping	sheet
Glue	metallic	Toothbrushes
Hole punch	textured	Toothpicks
Ink pads	tissue	Wire
Inking plate	wallpaper	Wood blocks
Magazines	watercolor	Yarn
Marbles	white drawing	

Appendix B

Activity Charts

For quick reference, a teacher or supervisor will be able to use the four activity charts that follow to find a suitable lesson to enhance classroom learning, based on subject matter, level, technique, or curriculum connection. The first chart, like this book, is arranged by the subject sample or theme. However, the subject can be changed according to the curriculum topic that is being reinforced in individual classrooms. Note that the activities could pertain to more than one theme. The activity titled Tree Mosaic is listed under the subject theme of trees, but the mosaic technique also qualifies it as a multicultural activity. The second chart is arranged by skill level, but the vocabulary and skill expectations can be simplified or enhanced to meet individual needs. The third chart is arranged according to technique, which might also be changed if alternate materials are being used. The fourth chart arranges the activities according to their suggested curriculum connections. It is important that the supervisors using these charts and the activities in this book realize that the more flexible they are in setting up and presenting the activities, the more satisfied they will be with the creativity and learning results of the children.

Guide to Chart Abbreviations

Level: **E** (easy), **M** (moderate), **A** (advanced)

Technique: **D** (drawing), **P** (painting), **Pr** (printing), **C and P** (cutting and pasting), **C** (cutting), **S** (sculpture)

Curriculum Connection: **M** (math), **LA** (language arts), **Sc** (science), **SS** (social studies), **PE** (physical education), **Mu** (music)

Activity Chart: Overview

Activity Title	Level	Technique	Curriculum Connection	Page Number
Design				
Dots and Dashes	E	D	M	15
Sock Puppets	E	D	LA, M	16
Scissors Design	M	D	M	17
Circles and Lines	E	D, C and P	M	18
Straight Line Design	M	D	M	19
Red Magic Ball	E	D	LA	20
Styrofoam Block Printing	M	D, Pr	Sc, M	21
Fruits or Vegetables				
Apple Design	M	D	Sc, M	22
Cut-Paper Still Life	M	D, C and P	Sc, SS, M	23
Fruit Still Life	E	P	Sc, SS, M	24
Grapevines	E	D, Pr	Sc, SS, M	25
Chalk Dipped in Paint Still Life	M	D	Sc, SS, M	26
Vegetable Print	E	Pr	Sc, SS, M	27
Food Face	M	C and P	Sc, SS	28
Neighborhood				
City Street	M	C and P, Pr	SS	29
Painted Buildings	E	P	SS, M, LA	30
Bus Field Trip	E	D	Sc, SS, LA	31
Creative Playground	E	C and P, S	SS, M, LA	32
Paper Bag House	M	S, C and P	Sc, SS, LA	33
Trees				
Tree Mosaic	A	C and P	Sc, SS, M	34
One-Point Perspective	A	D, P	Sc, M	35
Jungle or Rain Forest Scene	M	D, P	Sc, SS	36
Straw-Blown-Paint Tree	M	P, Pr	Sc, SS, LA	37
Winter Tree	M	P	Sc, SS	38
Crayon-Resist Fall Tree	E	P	Sc, SS	39
Long Tree	M	D	Sc, SS	40
Forest Trees	M	C and P	Sc, SS, M	41
Scratch Art Tree	A	D	Sc, SS	42
Positive and Negative Tree Design	A	D, C and P	Sc, SS	43
Leaves				
Styrofoam Printed Leaves	A	Pr	Sc, SS	44
Textured Leaves with Bugs	M	C and P, Pr	Sc, SS	45
Chalk-Line Leaves	E	D	Sc, SS	46
Watercolor Leaves	E	D, P	Sc, SS	47
Positive and Negative Leaves Design	M	D	Sc, SS, M	48
Flowers				
Silhouette with Crayon-Resist Design	M	C and P, D, P	Sc, M	49
Flower Garden	M	C and P	Sc, SS, M	50
Flower Transfer Drawing	E	D, Pr	Sc	51
Flower Print	E	Pr	Sc, M	52
Insects				
Clay Bugs	M	D, C, S	Sc, SS, M	53
Looking in the Grass with a Magnifying Glass	A	D	Sc	54
Caterpillars on Leaves	E	P, C and P	Sc, M	55

Activity Title	Level	Technique	Curriculum Connection	Page Number
Crayon Bugs with Watercolor Leaves	E	D, P	Sc, LA, M	56
Bugs in a Container	E	D	Sc, M	57
Mountains				
Textured Mountains	A	C and P, Pr	Sc, SS, M	58
Chalk Mountains	E	D	Sc, SS, M	59
Mountain Range	M	D, P	Sc, SS, M	60
Volcano Explosions	E	D, C and P	Sc, SS	61
Mountain Chalk Rubbings	E	C, Pr	Sc, SS	62
Sky				
Constellations	A	C and P	Sc, SS, M, LA	63
Star Gazers	M	D, C and P, Pr	Sc, SS, LA	64
Chalk-Stenciled Stars	M	Pr	Sc, M	65
Man in the Moon	M	S, C and P	Sc, SS, M	66
Sun Faces	E	D, P	Sc, M	67
Ocean				
Fish Tessellation	A	C and P, D, P	Sc, M	68
Quartered Fish	A	D, P	Sc, M	69
Tissue Paper Fish	M	C and P	Sc, SS	70
Fish Plaque	A	S, P	Sc, SS	71
Depths of the Ocean	A	P, C and P	Sc, SS, M	72
Aquarium Windsock	E	D, P	Sc, SS, M	73
People				
Sports Person	M	D, C and P	Sc, PE, M	74
Self-Portrait	E	C and P	Sc, LA	75
Cylinder Characters	M	C and P, S	LA, SS	76
Faces in the Crowd	E	D, P	Sc, LA	77
Neckties	M	D	SS, LA	78
Smiley Face	M	P, C and P, Pr	Sc, SS, LA	79
Electric Body Design	M	D	Sc, Mu	80
Looking Out the Window	M	D, P	Sc, M, LA	81
Stick Puppets	M	D, C and P	Sc, SS, LA	82
Paper Bag Puppet	M	S, C and P	Sc, SS, LA	83
Birds				
Colorful Bird	M	D	Sc, SS	84
Baby Owls	E	Pr, C and P	Sc, SS	85
Patterned Bird	M	D	Sc, SS, LA, M	86
Feathered Friends	M	C and P, P	Sc, SS	87
Clay Bird in Nest	E	S	Sc, SS	88
Tropical Bird Mobile	A	S, C and P	Sc, SS	89
Tall Birds	E	P	Sc, SS	90
Animals				
Animal Mosaics	A	C and P	Sc, SS, M	91
Zebra Skins	E	P	Sc, SS	92
Snakes	M	D	Sc, SS, M	93
Giraffes	M	P	Sc, SS, M	94
Giraffe	E	C and P, Pr	Sc, SS, M	95
Penguins	M	P	Sc, SS, M	96
Spider and Web	E	D, P	Sc, SS, LA, M	97
Painted Turtles	E	D, P	Sc, SS, M	98
Torn-Paper Animals	M	C and P	Sc, SS	99
Clay Animals	M	S	Sc, SS	100

Activity Title	Level	Technique	Curriculum Connection	Page Number
Dental Health				
Tooth Person Brushing Hair	M	C and P	Sc	101
Tooth Fairy	E	D, P	Sc	102
Flying Tooth Fairy	A	C and P, Pr	Sc	103
Newspaper in Education				
Painted Tree on Newspaper	E	P	Sc, SS, LA	104
Newspaper Masks	M	C and P	Sc, SS, LA	105
Person Reading	M	C and P	Sc, SS, LA	106
Seasonal				
Turkey	E	D, C and P, Pr	Sc, SS, M	107
Woven Scarecrow	A	C and P	Sc, SS, LA	108
Snowman in a Snowstorm	E	Pr, C and P	Sc, SS, M	109
Winter Scene	A	D, C and P, Pr	Sc, SS	110
Multicultural				
Paper Pottery	E	C and P, D	Sc, SS, M, LA	111
Dragons or Mythical Beasts	E	D	Sc, SS, LA	112
Positive and Negative Quilt	A	C and P	Sc, SS, M	113
Fraction Quilt	A	D	Sc, SS, M, LA	114
Textured Quilt	E	P, Pr	Sc, SS, M	115
Fireworks Celebration	A	D, C and P	Sc, SS, LA	116

Activity Chart: Level

Activity Level	Subject	Technique	Curriculum Connection	Page Number
Easy				
Dots and Dashes	Design	D	M	15
Sock Puppets	Design	D	LA, M	16
Circles and Lines	Design	D, C and P	M	18
Red Magic Ball	Design	D	LA	20
Fruit Still Life	Fruit or Vegetables	P	Sc, SS, M	24
Grapevines	Fruit or Vegetables	D, Pr	Sc, SS, M	25
Vegetable Print	Fruit or Vegetables	Pr	Sc, SS, M	27
Painted Buildings	Neighborhood	P	SS, M, LA	30
Bus Field Trip	Neighborhood	D	Sc, SS, LA	31
Creative Playground	Neighborhood	C and P, S	SS, M, LA	32
Crayon-Resist Fall Tree	Trees	P	Sc, SS	39
Chalk-Line Leaves	Leaves	D	Sc, SS	46
Watercolor Leaves	Leaves	D, P	Sc, SS	47
Flower Transfer Drawing	Flowers	D, Pr	Sc	
Flower Print	Flowers	Pr	Sc, M	52
Caterpillars on Leaves	Insects	P, C and P	Sc, M	55
Crayon Bugs with Watercolor Leaves	Insects	D, P	Sc, LA, M	56
Bugs in a Container	Insects	D	Sc, M	57
Chalk Mountains	Mountains	D	Sc, SS, M	59
Volcano Explosions	Mountains	D, C and P	Sc, SS	61
Mountain Chalk Rubbings	Mountains	C, Pr	Sc, SS	62
Sun Faces	Sky	D, P	Sc, M	67
Aquarium Windsock	Ocean	D, P	Sc, SS, M	73
Self-Portrait	People	C and P	Sc, LA	75
Faces in the Crowd	People	D, P	Sc, LA	77
Baby Owls	Birds	Pr, C and P	Sc, SS	85
Clay Bird in Nest	Birds	S	Sc, SS	88
Tall Birds	Birds	P	Sc, SS	90
Zebra Skins	Animals	P	Sc, SS	92
Giraffe	Animals	C and P, Pr	Sc, SS, M	95
Spider and Web	Animals	D, P	Sc, SS, M	97
Painted Turtles	Animals	D, P	Sc, SS, M	98
Tooth Fairy	Dental Health	D, P	Sc	102
Painted Tree on Newspaper	Newspaper in Education	P	Sc, SS, LA	104
Turkey	Seasonal	D, C and P, Pr	Sc, SS, M	107
Snowman in a Snowstorm	Seasonal	Pr, C and P	Sc, SS, M	109
Paper Pottery	Multicultural	C and P, D	Sc, SS, M, LA	
Dragons or Mythical Beasts	Multicultural	D	Sc, SS, LA	112
Textured Quilt	Multiculutural	P, Pr	Sc, SS, M	115
Moderate				
Scissors Design	Design	D	M	17
Straight Line Design	Design	D	M	19
Styrofoam Block Printing	Design	D, Pr	Sc, M	21
Apple Design	Fruit or Vegetable	D	Sc, M	22
Cut-Paper Still Life	Fruit or Vegetable	D, C and P	Sc, SS, M	23
Chalk Dipped in Paint Still Life	Fruit or Vegetable	D	Sc, SS, M	26
Food Face	Fruit or Vegetable	C and P	Sc, SS	28
City Street	Neighborhood	C and P, Pr	SS	29

125

Activity Level	Subject	Technique	Curriculum Connection	Page Number
Paper Bag House	Neighborhood	S, C and P	Sc, SS, LA	33
Jungle or Rain Forest Scene	Trees	D, P	Sc, SS	36
Straw-Blown-Paint Tree	Trees	P, Pr	Sc, SS, LA	37
Winter Tree	Trees	P	Sc, SS	38
Long Tree	Trees	D	Sc, SS	40
Forest Trees	Trees	C and P	Sc, Ss, M	41
Textured Leaves with Bugs	Leaves	C and P, Pr	Sc, SS	45
Positive and Negative Leaves Design	Leaves	D	Sc, SS, M	48
Silhouette with Crayon-Resist Design	Flowers	C and P, D, P	Sc, M	49
Flower Garden	Flowers	C and P	Sc, SS, M	50
Clay Bugs	Insects	D, C, S	Sc, SS, M	53
Mountain Range	Mountains	D, P	Sc, SS, M	60
Star Gazers	Sky	D, C and P, Pr	Sc, SS, LA	64
Chalk-Stenciled Stars	Sky	Pr	Sc, M	65
Man in the Moon	Sky	S, C and P	Sc, SS, M	66
Tissue Paper Fish	Ocean	C and P	Sc, SS	70
Sports Person	People	D, C and P	Sc, PE, M	74
Cylinder Characters	People	C and P, S	LA, SS	76
Neckties	People	D	SS, LA	78
Smiley Face	People	P, C and P, Pr	Sc, SS, LA	79
Electric Body Design	People	D	Sc, Mu	80
Looking Out the Window	People	D, P	Sc, M, LA	81
Stick Puppets	People	D, C and P	Sc, SS, LA	82
Paper Bag Puppet	People	S, C and P	Sc, SS, LA	83
Colorful Bird	Birds	D	Sc, SS	84
Patterned Bird	Birds	D	Sc, SS, LA, M	86
Feathered Friends	Birds	C and P, P	Sc, SS	87
Snakes	Animals	D	Sc, SS, M	93
Giraffes	Animals	P	Sc, SS, M	94
Penguins	Animals	P	Sc, SS, M	96
Torn-Paper Animals	Animals	C and P	Sc, SS	99
Clay Animals	Animals	S	Sc, SS	100
Tooth Person Brushing Hair	Dental Health	C and P	Sc	101
Newspaper Masks	Newspaper in Education	C and P	Sc, SS, LA	105
Person Reading	Newspaper in Education	C and P	Sc, SS, LA	106
Advanced				
Tree Mosaic	Trees	C and P	Sc, SS, M	34
One-Point Perspective	Trees	D, P	Sc, M	35
Scratch Art Tree	Trees	D	Sc, SS	42
Positive and Negative Tree Design	Trees	D, C and P	Sc, SS	43
Styrofoam Printed Leaves	Leaves	Pr	Sc, SS	44
Looking in the Grass with a Magnifying Glass	Insects	D	Sc	54
Textured Mountains	Mountains	C and P, Pr	Sc, SS, M	58
Constellations	Sky	C and P	Sc, SS, M, LA	63
Fish Tessellation	Ocean	C and P, D, P	Sc, M	68

Activity Level	Subject	Technique	Curriculum Connection	Page Number
Quartered Fish	Ocean	D, P	Sc, M	69
Fish Plaque	Ocean	S, P	Sc, SS	71
Depths of the Ocean	Ocean	P, C and P	Sc, SS, M	72
Tropical Bird Mobile	Birds	S, C and P	Sc, SS	89
Animal Mosaics	Animals	C and P	Sc, SS, M	91
Flying Tooth Fairy	Dental Health	C and P, Pr	Sc	103
Woven Scarecrow	Seasonal	C and P	Sc, SS, LA	108
Winter Scene	Seasonal	D, C and P, Pr	Sc, SS	110
Positive and Negative Quilt	Multicultural	C and P	Sc, SS, M	113
Fraction Quilt	Multicultural	D	Sc, SS, M, LA	114
Fireworks Celebration	Multicultural	D, C and P	Sc, SS, LA	116

Activity Chart: Technique

Activity Technique	Subject	Level	Curriculum Connection	Page Number
Drawing				
Dots and Dashes	Design	E	M	15
Sock Puppets	Design	E	LA, M	16
Circles and Lines	Design	E	M	18
Red Magic Ball	Design	E	LA	20
Grapevines	Fruit or Vegetables	E	Sc, SS, M	25
Bus Field Trip	Neighborhood	E	Sc, SS, LA	31
Chalk-Line Leaves	Leaves	E	Sc, M	46
Watercolor Leaves	Leaves	E	Sc, M	47
Flower Transfer Drawing	Flowers	E	Sc	5151
Crayon Bugs with Watercolor Leaves	Insects	E	Sc, LA, M	56
Bugs in a Container	Insects	E	Sc, M	57
Chalk Mountains	Mountains	E	Sc, SS, M	59
Volcano Explosions	Mountains	E	Sc, M	61
Sun Faces	Sky	E	Sc, M	67
Aquarium Windsock	Ocean	E	Sc, SS, M	73
Faces in the Crowd	People	E	Sc, LA	77
Spider and Web	Animals	E	Sc, SS, LA, M	97
Painted Turtles	Animals	E	Sc, SS, M	98
Tooth Fairy	Dental Health	E	Sc	102
Turkey	Seasonal	E	Sc, SS, M	107
Paper Pottery	Multicultural	E	Sc, SS, M, LA	111
Dragons or Mythical Beasts	Multicultural	E	Sc, SS, LA	112
Scissors Design	Design	M	M	17
Straight Line Design	Design	M	M	19
Styrofoam Block Printing	Design	M	Sc, M	21
Apple Design	Fruit or Vegetables	M	Sc, M	22
Cut-Paper Still Life	Fruit or Vegetables	M	Sc, SS, M	23
Chalk Dipped in Paint Still Life	Fruit or Vegetables	M	Sc, SS, M	26
Jungle or Rain Forest Scene	Trees	M	Sc, SS	36
Long Tree	Trees	M	Sc, M	40
Positive and Negative Leaves Design	Leaves	M	Sc, SS, M	48
Silhouette with Crayon-Resist Design	Flowers	M	Sc, SS	49
Clay Bugs	Insects	M	Sc, SS, M	53
Mountain Range	Mountains	M	Sc, SS, M	60
Star Gazers	Sky	M	Sc, SS, LA	64
Sports Person	People	M	Sc, PE, M	74
Neckties	People	M	SS, LA	78
Electric Body Design	People	M	Sc, Mu	80
Looking Out the Window	People	M	Sc, M, LA	81
Stick Puppets	People	M	Sc, SS, LA	82
Colorful Bird	Birds	M	Sc, SS	84
Patterned Bird	Birds	M	Sc, SS, LA, M	86
Snakes	Animals	M	Sc, SS, M	93
One-Point Perspective	Trees	A	Sc, M	35
Scratch Art Tree	Trees	A	Sc, SS	42
Positive and Negative Tree Design	Trees	A	Sc, SS	43
Looking in the Grass with a Magnifying Glass	Insects	A	Sc	54

Activity Technique	Subject	Level	Curriculum Connection	Page Number
Fish Tessellation	Ocean	A	Sc, M	68
Quartered Fish	Ocean	A	Sc, M	69
Winter Scene	Seasonal	A	Sc, SS	110
Fraction Quilt	Multicultural	A	Sc, SS, M, LA	114
Fireworks Celebration	Multicultural	A	Sc, SS, LA	116
Cutting and Pasting				
Circles and Lines	Design	E	M	18
Creative Playground	Neighborhood	E	SS, M, LA	32
Caterpillars on Leaves	Insects	E	Sc, M	55
Volcano Explosions	Mountains	E	Sc, SS	61
Mountain Chalk Rubbings	Mountains	E	Sc, SS	62
Self-Portrait	People	E	Sc, LA	75
Baby Owls	Birds	E	Sc, SS	85
Giraffe	Animals	E	Sc, SS, M	95
Turkey	Seasonal	E	Sc, SS, M	107
Snowman in a Snowstorm	Seasonal	E	Sc, SS, M	109
Paper Pottery	Multicultural	E	Sc, SS, M, LA	111
Cut-Paper Still Life	Fruit or Vegetables	M	Sc, SS, M	23
Food Face	Fruit or Vegetables	M	Sc, SS	28
City Street	Neighborhood	M	SS	29
Paper Bag House	Neighborhood	M	Sc, SS, LA	33
Forest Trees	Trees	M	Sc, SS, M	41
Textured Leaves with Bugs	Leaves	M	Sc, SS	45
Silhouette with Crayon-Resist Design	Flowers	M	Sc, M	49
Flower Garden	Flowers	M	Sc, SS, M	50
Clay Bugs	Insects	M	Sc, SS, M	53
Star Gazers	Sky	M	Sc, SS, LA	64
Man in the Moon	Sky	M	Sc, SS, M	66
Tissue Paper Fish	Ocean	M	Sc, SS	70
Sports Person	People	M	Sc, PE, M	74
Cylinder Characters	People	M	LA, SS	76
Smiley Face	People	M	Sc, SS, LA	79
Stick Puppets	People	M	Sc, SS, LA	82
Paper Bag Puppet	People	M	Sc, SS, LA	83
Feathered Friends	Birds	M	Sc, SS	87
Torn-Paper Animals	Animals	M	Sc, SS	99
Tooth Person Brushing Hair	Dental Health	M	Sc	101
Newspaper Masks	Newspaper in Education	M	Sc, SS, LA	105
Person Reading	Newspaper in Education	M	Sc, SS, LA	106
Tree Mosaic	Trees	A	Sc, SS, M	34
Positive and Negative Tree Design	Trees	A	Sc, SS	43
Textured Mountains	Mountains	A	Sc, SS, M	58
Constellations	Sky	A	Sc, SS, M, LA	63
Fish Tessellation	Ocean	A	Sc, M	68
Depths of the Ocean	Ocean	A	Sc, SS, M	72
Tropical Bird Mobile	Birds	A	Sc, SS	89
Animal Mosaics	Animals	A	Sc, SS, M	91
Flying Tooth Fairy	Dental Health	A	Sc	103

Activity Technique	Subject	Level	Curriculum Connection	Page Number
Woven Scarecrow	Seasonal	A	Sc, SS, LA	108
Winter Scene	Seasonal	A	Sc, SS	110
Positive and Negative Quilt	Multicultural	A	Sc, SS, M	113
Fireworks Celebration	Multicultural	A	Sc, SS, LA	116
Painting				
Fruit Still Life	Fruit or Vegetables	E	Sc, SS, M	24
Painted Buildings	Neighborhood	E	SS, M, LA	30
Crayon-Resist Fall Tree	Trees	E	Sc, SS	39
Watercolor Leaves	Leaves	E	Sc, SS	47
Caterpillars on Leaves	Insects	E	Sc, M	55
Crayon Bugs with Watercolor Leaves	Insects	E	Sc, LA, M	56
Sun Faces	Sky	E	Sc, M	67
Aquarium Windsock	Ocean	E	Sc, SS, M	73
Faces in the Crowd	People	E	Sc, LA	77
Tall Birds	Birds	E	Sc, SS	90
Zebra Skins	Animals	E	Sc, SS	92
Spider and Web	Animals	E	Sc, SS, LA, M	97
Painted Turtles	Animals	E	Sc, SS, M	98
Tooth Fairy	Dental Health	E	Sc	102
Painted Tree on Newspaper	Newspaper in Education	E	Sc, SS, LA	104
Textured Quilt	Multicultural	E	Sc, SS, M	115
Jungle or Rain Forest Scene	Trees	M	Sc, SS	36
Straw-Blown-Paint Tree	Trees	M	Sc, Ss, LA	37
Winter Tree	Trees	M	Sc, SS	38
Silhouette with Crayon-Resist Design	Flowers	M	Sc, M	49
Mountain Range	Mountains	M	Sc, SS, M	60
Smiley Face	People	M	Sc, SS, LA	79
Looking Out the Window	People	M	Sc, M, LA	81
Feathered Friends	Birds	M	Sc, SS	87
Giraffes	Animals	M	Sc, SS, M	94
Penguins	Animals	M	Sc, SS, M	96
One-Point Perspective	Trees	A	Sc, M	35
Fish Tessellation	Ocean	A	Sc, M	
Quartered Fish	Ocean	A	Sc, M	69
Fish Plaque	Ocean	A	Sc, SS	71
Depths of the Ocean	Ocean	A	Sc, SS, M	72
Printing				
Grapevines	Fruit or Vegetables	E	Sc, SS, M	25
Vegetable Print	Fruit or Vegetables	E	Sc, SS, M	27
Flower Transfer Drawing	Flowers	E	Sc	51
Flower Print	Flowers	E	Sc, M	52
Mountain Chalk Rubbings	Mountains	E	Sc, SS	62
Baby Owls	Birds	E	Sc, SS	85
Giraffe	Animals	E	Sc, SS, M	95
Turkey	Seasonal	E	Sc, SS, M	107
Snowman in a Snowstorm	Seasonal	E	Sc, SS, M	109
Textured Quilt	Multicultural	E	Sc, SS, M	115
Styrofoam Block Printing	Design	M	Sc, M	21
City Street	Neighborhood	M	SS	29
Straw-Blown-Paint Tree	Trees	M	Sc, SS, LA	37

Activity Technique	Subject	Level	Curriculum Connection	Page Number
Textured Leaves with Bugs	Leaves	M	Sc, SS	45
Star Gazers	Sky	M	Sc, SS, LA	64
Chalk-Stenciled Stars	Sky	M	Sc, M	65
Smiley Face	People	M	Sc, SS, LA	79
Styrofoam Printed Leaves	Leaves	A	Sc, SS	44
Textured Mountains	Mountains	A	Sc, SS, M	58
Winter Scene	Seasonal	A	Sc, SS	110
Sculpture				
Creative Playground	Neighborhood	E	SS, M, LA	32
Clay Bird in Nest	Birds	E	Sc, SS	88
Paper Bag House	Neighborhood	M	Sc, SS, LA	33
Clay Bugs	Insects	M	Sc, SS, M	53
Man in the Moon	Sky	M	Sc, SS, M	66
Cylinder Characters	People	M	LA, SS	76
Paper Bag Puppet	People	M	Sc, SS, LA	83
Clay Animals	Animals	M	Sc, SS	100
Fish Plaque	Ocean	A	Sc, SS	71
Tropical Bird Mobile	Birds	A	Sc, SS	89

Activity Chart: Curriculum Connection

Activity Curriculum Connection	Subject	Technique	Level	Page Number
Math				
Dots and Dashes	Design	D	E	15
Sock Puppets	Design	D	E	16
Circles and Lines	Design	D, C and P	E	18
Fruit Still Life	Fruit or Vegetables	P	E	24
Grapevines	Fruit or Vegetables	D, Pr	E	25
Vegetable Print	Fruit or Vegetables	Pr	E	27
	30	Neighborhood	P	E
Creative Playground	Neighborhood	C and P, S	E	32
Flower Print	Flowers	Pr	E	52
Caterpillars on Leaves	Insects	P, C and P	E	55
Crayon Bugs with Watercolor Leaves	Insects	D, P	E	56
Bugs in a Container	Insects	D	E	57
Chalk Mountains	Mountains	D	E	59
Sun Faces	Sky	D, P	E	67
Aquarium Windsock	Ocean	D, P	E	73
Giraffe	Animals	C and P, Pr	E	95
Spider and Web	Animals	D, P	E	97
Painted Turtles	Animals	D, P	E	98
Turkey	Seasonal	D, C and P, Pr	E	107
Snowman in a Snowstorm	Seasonal	Pr, C and P	E	109
Paper Pottery	Multicultural	C and P, D	E	111
Textured Quilt	Multicultural	P, Pr	E	115
Scissors Design	Design	D	M	17
Straight Line Design	Design	D	M	19
Styrofoam Block Printing	Design	D, Pr	M	21
Apple Design	Fruit or Vegetables	D	M	22
Cut-Paper Still Life	Fruit or Vegetables	D, C and P	M	23
Chalk Dipped in Paint Still Life	Fruit or Vegetables	D	M	26
Forest Trees	Trees	C and P	M	41
Positive and Negative Leaves Design	Leaves	D	M	48
Silhouette with Crayon-Resist Design	Flowers	C and P, D, P	M	49
Flower Garden	Flowers	C and P	M	50
Clay Bugs	Insects	D, C, S	M	53
Mountain Range	Mountains	D, P	M	60
Chalk-Stenciled Stars	Sky	Pr	M	65
Man in the Moon	Sky	S, C and P	M	66
Sports Person	People	D, C and P	M	74
Looking Out the Window	People	D, P	M	81
Patterned Bird	Birds	D	M	86
Snakes	Animals	D	M	93
Giraffes	Animals	P	M	94
Penguins	Animals	P	M	96
Tree Mosaic	Trees	C and P	A	34
One-Point Perspective	Trees	D, P	A	35
Textured Mountains	Mountains	C and P, Pr	A	58
Constellations	Sky	C and P	A	63
Fish Tessellation	Ocean	C and P, D, P	A	68

Activity Curriculum Connection	Subject	Technique	Level	Page Number
Quartered Fish	Ocean	D, P	A	69
Depths of the Ocean	Ocean	P, C and P	A	72
Animal Mosaics	Animals	C and P	A	91
Positive and Negative Quilt	Multicultural	C and P	A	113
Fraction Quilt	Multicultural	D	A	114
Language Arts				
Sock Puppets	Design	D	E	16
Red Magic Ball	Design	D	E	20
Painted Buildings	Neighborhood	P	E	30
Bus Field Trip	Neighborhood	D	E	31
Creative Playground	Neighborhood	C and P, S	E	32
Crayon Bugs with Watercolor Leaves	Insects	D, P	E	56
Self-Portrait	People	C and P	E	75
Faces in the Crowd	People	D, P	E	77
Spider and Web	Animals	D, P	E	97
Painted Tree on Newspaper	Newspaper in Education	P	E	104
Paper Pottery	Multicultural	C and P, D	E	111
Dragons or Mythical Beasts	Multicultural	D	E	112
Paper Bag House	Neighborhood	S, C and P	M	33
Straw-Blown-Paint Tree	Trees	P, Pr	M	37
Star Gazers	Sky	D, C and P, Pr	M	64
Cylinder Characters	People	C and P, S	M	76
Neckties	People	D	M	78
Smiley Face	People	P, C and P, Pr	M	79
Looking Out the Window	People	D, P	M	81
Stick Puppets	People	D, C and P	M	82
Paper Bag Puppet	People	S, C and P	M	83
Patterned Bird	Birds	D	M	86
Newspaper Masks	Newspaper in Education	C and P	M	105
Person Reading	Newspaper in Education	C and P	106	M
Constellations	Sky	C and P	A	63
Woven Scarecrow	Seasonal	C and P	A	108
Fraction Quilt	Multicultural	D	A	114
Fireworks Celebration	Multicultural	D, C and P	A	116
Science				
Fruit Still Life	Fruit or Vegetables	P	E	24
Grapevines	Fruit or Vegetables	D, Pr	E	25
Vegetable Print	Fruit or Vegetables	Pr	E	27
Bus Field Trip	Neighborhood	D	E	31
Crayon-Resist Fall Tree	Trees	P	E	39
Chalk-Line Leaves	Leaves	D	E	46
Watercolor Leaves	Leaves	D, P	E	47
Flower Transfer Drawing	Flowers	D, Pr	E	51
Flower Print	Flowers	Pr	E	52
Caterpillars on Leaves	Insects	P, C and P	E	55
Crayon Bugs with Watercolor Leaves	Insects	D, P	E	56
Bugs in a Container	Insects	D	E	57

Activity Curriculum Connection	Subject	Technique	Level	Page Number
Chalk Mountains	Mountains	D	E	59
Volcano Explosions	Mountains	D, C and P	E	61
Mountain Chalk Rubbings	Mountains	C, Pr	E	62
Sun Faces	Sky	D, P	E	67
Aquarium Windsock	Ocean	D, P	E	73
Self-Portrait	People	C and P	E	75
Faces in the Crowd	People	D, P	E	77
Baby Owls	Birds	Pr, C and P	E	85
Clay Bird in Nest	Birds	S	E	88
Tall Birds	Birds	P	E	90
Zebra Skins	Animals	P	E	92
Giraffe	Animals	C and P, Pr	E	95
Spider and Web	Animals	D, P	E	97
Painted Turtles	Animals	D, P	E	98
Tooth Fairy	Dental Health	D, P	E	102
Painted Tree on Newspaper	Newspaper in Education	P	E	104
Turkey	Seasonal	D, C and P, Pr	E	107
Snowman in a Snowstorm	Seasonal	Pr, C and P	E	109
Paper Pottery	Multicultural	C and P, D	E	111
Dragons or Mythical Beasts	Multicultural	D	E	112
Textured Quilt	Multicultural	P, Pr	E	115
Styrofoam Block Printing	Design	D, Pr	M	21
Apple Design	Fruit or Vegetables	D	M	22
Cut-Paper Still Life	Fruit or Vegetables	D, C and P	M	23
Chalk Dipped in Paint Still Life	Fruit or Vegetables	D	M	26
Food Face	Fruit or Vegetables	C and P	M	28
Paper Bag House	Neighborhood	S, C and P	M	33
Jungle or Rain Forest Scene	Trees	D, P	M	36
Straw-Blown-Paint Tree	Trees	P, Pr	M	37
Winter Tree	Trees	P	M	38
Long Tree	Trees	D	M	40
Forest Trees	Trees	C and P	M	41
Textured Leaves with Bugs	Leaves	C and P, Pr	M	45
Positive and Negative Leaves Design	Leaves	D	M	48
Silhouette with Crayon-Resist Design	Flowers	C and P, D, P	M	49
Flower Garden	Flowers	C and P	M	50
Clay Bugs	Insects	D, C, S	M	53
Mountain Range	Mountains	D, P	M	60
Star Gazers	Sky	D, C and P, Pr	M	64
Chalk-Stenciled Stars	Sky	Pr	M	65
Man in the Moon	Sky	S, C and P	M	66
Tissue Paper Fish	Ocean	C and P	M	70
Sports Person	People	D, C and P	M	74
Smiley Face	People	P, C and P, Pr	M	79
Electric Body Design	People	D	M	80
Looking Out the Window	People	D, P	M	81
Stick Puppets	People	D, C and P	M	82
Paper Bag Puppet	People	S, C and P	M	83

Activity Curriculum Connection	Subject	Technique	Level	Page Number
Colorful Bird	Birds	D	M	84
Patterned Bird	Birds	D	M	86
Feathered Friends	Birds	C and P, P	M	87
Snakes	Animals	D	M	93
Giraffes	Animals	P	M	94
Penguins	Animals	P	M	96
Torn-Paper Animals	Animals	C and P	M	99
Clay Animals	Animals	S	M	100
Tooth Person Brushing Hair	Dental Health	C and P	M	101
Newspaper Masks	Newspaper in Education	C and P	M	105
Person Reading	Newspaper in Education	C and P	M	106
Tree Mosaic	Trees	C and P	A	34
One-Point Perspective	Trees	D, P	A	35
Scratch Art Tree	Trees	D	A	42
Positive and Negative Tree Design	Trees	D, C and P	A	43
Styrofoam Printed Leaves	Leaves	Pr	A	44
Looking in the Grass with a Magnifying Glass	Insects	D	A	54
Textured Mountains	Mountains	C and P, Pr	A	58
Constellations	Sky	C and P	A	63
Fish Tessellation	Ocean	C and P, D, P	A	68
Quartered Fish	Ocean	D, P	A	69
Fish Plaque	Ocean	S, P	A	71
Depths of the Ocean	Ocean	P, C and P	A	72
Tropical Bird Mobile	Birds	S, C and P	A	89
Animal Mosaics	Animals	C and P	A	91
Flying Tooth Fairy	Dental Health	C and P, Pr	A	103
Woven Scarecrow	Seasonal	C and P	A	108
Winter Scene	Seasonal	D, C and P, Pr	A	110
Positive and Negative Quilt	Multicultural	C and P	A	113
Fraction Quilt	Multicultural	D	A	114
Fireworks Celebration	Multicultural	D, C and P	A	116

Social Studies

Fruit Still Life	Fruit or Vegetables	P	E	24
Grapevines	Fruit or Vegetables	D, Pr	E	25
Vegetable Print	Fruit or Vegetables	Pr	E	27
Painted Buildings	Neighborhood	P	E	30
Bus Field Trip	Neighborhood	D	E	31
Creative Playground	Neighborhood	C and P, S	E	32
Crayon-Resist Fall Tree	Trees	P	E	39
Chalk-Line Leaves	Leaves	D	E	46
Watercolor Leaves	Leaves	D, P	E	47
Chalk Mountains	Mountains	D, P	E	59
Volcano Explosions	Mountains	D, C and P	E	61
Mountain Chalk Rubbings	Mountains	C, Pr	E	62
Aquarium Windsock	Ocean	D, P	E	73
Baby Owls	Birds	Pr, C and P	E	85
Clay Bird in Nest	Birds	S	E	88
Tall Birds	Birds	P	E	90

Activity Curriculum Connection	Subject	Technique	Level	Page Number
Zebra Skins	Animals	P	E	92
Giraffe	Animals	C and P, Pr	E	95
Spider and Web	Animals	D, P	E	97
Painted Turtles	Animals	D, P	E	98
Painted Tree on Newspaper	Newspaper in Education	P	E	104
Turkey	Seasonal	D, C and P, Pr	E	107
Snowman in a Snowstorm	Seasonal	Pr, C and P	E	109
Paper Pottery	Multicultural	C and P, D	E	111
Dragons or Mythical Beasts	Multicultural	D	E	112
Textured Quilt	Multicultural	P, Pr	E	115
Cut-Paper Still Life	Fruit or Vegetables	D, C and P	M	23
Chalk Dipped in Paint Still Life	Fruit or Vegetables	D	M	26
Food Face	Fruit or Vegetables	C and P	M	28
City Street	Neighborhood	C and P, Pr	M	29
Paper Bag House	Neighborhood	S, C and P	M	33
Jungle or Rain Forest Scene	Trees	D, P	M	36
Straw-Blown-Paint Tree	Trees	P, Pr	M	37
Winter Tree	Trees	P	M	38
Long Tree	Trees	D	M	40
Forest Trees	Trees	C and P	M	41
Textured Leaves with Bugs	Leaves	C and P, Pr	M	45
Positive and Negative Leaves Design	Leaves	D	M	48
Flower Garden	Flowers	C and P	M	50
Clay Bugs	Insects	D, C, S	M	53
Mountain Range	Mountains	D, P	M	60
Star Gazers	Sky	D, C and P, Pr	M	64
Man in the Moon	Sky	S, C and P	M	66
Tissue Paper Fish	Ocean	C and P	M	70
Cylinder Characters	People	C and P, S	M	76
Neckties	People	D	M	78
Smiley Face	People	P, C and P, Pr	M	79
Stick Puppets	People	D, C and P	M	82
Paper Bag Puppet	People	S, C and P	M	83
Colorful Bird	Birds	D	M	84
Patterned Bird	Birds	D	M	86
Feathered Friends	Birds	C and P, P	M	87
Snakes	Animals	D	M	93
Giraffes	Animals	P	M	94
Penguins	Animals	P	M	96
Torn-Paper Animals	Animals	C and P	M	99
Clay Animals	Animals	S	M	100
Newspaper Masks	Newspaper in Education	C and P	M	105
Person Reading	Newspaper in Education	C and P	M	106
Tree Mosaic	Trees	C and P	A	34
Scratch Art Tree	Trees	D	A	42
Positive and Negative Tree Design	Trees	D, C and P	A	43
Styrofoam Printed Leaves	Leaves	Pr	A	44

Activity Curriculum Connection	Subject	Technique	Level	Page Number
Textured Mountains	Mountains	C and P, Pr	A	58
Constellations	Sky	C and P	A	63
Fish Plaque	Ocean	S, P	A	71
Depths of the Ocean	Ocean	P, C and P	A	72
Tropical Bird Mobile	Birds	S, C and P	A	89
Animal Mosaics	Animals	C and P	A	91
Woven Scarecrow	Seasonal	C and P	A	108
Winter Scene	Seasonal	D, C and P, Pr	A	110
Positive and Negative Quilt	Multicultural	C and P	A	113
Fraction Quilt	Multicultural	D	A	114
Fireworks Celebration	Multicultural	D, C and P	A	116

Physical Education

Sports Person	People	D, C and P	M	74

Music

Electric Body Design	People	D	M	80

References

Art for Bangor elementary schools. (1976). Bangor, ME: Bangor School Department.

Arts and activities. San Diego: Publishers' Development Corp.

Chapman, L. (1985). *Discover art.* Worcester, MA: Davis.

Crayola creativity program. (1987). Easton, PA: Binney & Smith.

Horn, G. F., and Smith, G. S. (1971). *Experiencing art in the elementary school.* Dallas: Hendrick-Long and Worcester, MA: Davis.

Jenkins, P.D. (1980). *Art for the fun of it.* New York: Simon & Schuster.

Lansing, K. M., and Richards, A. E. (1981). *The elementary teacher's art handbook.* New York: Holt, Rinehart and Winston.

Libby, W. M. L. (2000). *Using art to make art.* Albany: Delmar/Thompson Learning.

School arts. Worcester, MA: Davis.

Wachowiak, F., and Ramsay, T. (1971). *Emphasis: ART.* Scranton, PA: Intext Educational Publishers.

Wankelman, W. F., Wigg, P., and Wigg, M. (1974). *A handbook of arts and crafts.* Dubuque, IA: Wm. C. Brown.

Glossary

abstract art—A visual interpretation with little regard to realistic representation.

aesthetic—Appreciation of the beauty in art or nature.

art appreciation—Awareness of the aesthetic values in artwork.

art medium—Material used to create an artwork.

art museum—A building where artwork is displayed.

art reproduction—Photographic duplication of an original piece of art.

asymmetrical—Artwork that looks balanced when the parts are arranged differently on each side.

background—The part of an artwork that looks farther away or is behind other parts.

balance—The arrangement of visual elements so that the parts seem to be equally important.

basic shapes—Circle, square, triangle, rectangle.

brayer—A roller used to apply paint or ink.

cityscape—A view or picture of a city.

collage—Artwork made by assembling and gluing materials to a flat surface.

composition—The arrangement of design elements in an artwork.

concept—A general idea or understanding.

construct—To create an artwork by putting materials together.

contour—The outline of a shape or form.

contrast—Difference between two things.

cool colors—Colors that remind the viewer of cool things. They often create a calm or sad feeling (blue, green, and purple).

crayon etching—Scratching through one layer of crayon to let another layer of crayon show through.

creative—The ability to make things in a new or different way.

Cubism—A style of art where shapes or forms seem to be divided or have many edges.

design—The ordered arrangement of art elements in an artwork.

design elements—Line, shape, form, texture, space, color, value.

design principles—Balance, emphasis, variety, unity, movement, rhythm, repetition.

detail—Small item or part of an artwork.

drawing—Describing something by means of line.

emphasis—Special stress of one or more art design components.

Expressionism—A style of art where a definite mood or feeling is depicted.

Fantasy Art—Artwork that is meant to look unreal, strange, or dreamlike.

foreground—The part in an artwork that seems near or close.

form—A three-dimensional design.

free form—A free-flowing, imaginative shape.

geometric shapes—Shapes that have smooth, regular edges.

horizontal—A line that goes from side to side.

illusion—A misleading image.

imagination—Creative thinking ability.

intermediate colors—Colors that are made by mixing a primary color and a secondary color (red-orange, red-violet, blue-green, blue-violet, yellow-orange, yellow-green).

landscape—Artwork that depicts an outdoor scene.

line—A mark made by a moving point.

mixed media—Artwork made up of different materials or techniques.

mobile—A sculpture with parts that move by air currents.

model—A person who poses for an artist.

montage—A composite picture made by combining several separate pictures.

mosaic—Artwork made with small pieces.

movement—The rhythmic qualities of a design.

mural—A large art work created or displayed on a wall.

negative space—Empty space in a design.

neutral colors—Brown, black, white and gray.

Nonobjective—A style of art created with colors, lines, and shapes, not objects or scenes.

opaque—Not transparent.

original—Artwork that looks very different from other artwork.

overlap—One part that covers some of another part.

pattern—Lines, colors, or shapes repeated in a planned way. A model or guide for making something.

perspective—Found in artwork in which the shapes of objects and distances between them look familiar or correct.

Pop Art—A style of art that uses everyday objects as the subject.

portrait—Artwork that depicts the face of a person.

positive space—The actual shapes or figures in a design.

pose—A specific position of the body.

primary colors—Colors from which other colors can be made (red, blue, and yellow)

print—To create an image by pressing and lifting something with ink or paint on it.

profile—The side view of a person or object.

proportion—The size, location, or amount of a part as compared to another part or the whole.

radial—Lines or shapes that come out from the center point.

Realism—A style of artwork that depicts objects or scenes as they appear in everyday life.

relief—Something that stands out from a flat background.

repetition—The repeated use of the same design elements.

Renaissance—A time in European history (1400–1600) after the Middle Ages. Artists during this time discovered many new ways to create things.

rhythm—A repetition of design elements to create a visual balance.

Romantic—A style of artwork that depicts adventures, imaginary events, faraway places, or strong feelings.

secondary colors—Colors that can be mixed from two primary colors (orange, green, and purple).

shade—The darkness of a color; a color mixed with black.

shape—The outline edge or flat surface of a form.

space—An empty place or area.

stencil—A flat material with a cutout design.

still life—An artwork that depicts nonliving objects.

style—An artist's individual way of creating art.

symmetry—Parts arranged the same way on both sides.

technique—A specific way to create artwork.

tesselation—A repeating design that covers an infinite geometric plane without gaps or overlaps.

texture—The way something feels or the way it looks like it feels.

three-dimensional—Artwork that can be measured three ways: height, width, and depth.

tint—A lightened color, a color mixed with white.

transparent—Transmitting light, see-through.

two-dimensional—Artwork that is flat and measured in two ways: height and width.

unity—The quality of having all parts of an artwork look like they belong together.

value—The lightness or darkness of a color.

variety—Having differences.

vertical—A line that runs up and down.

warm colors—Colors that remind the viewer of warm things (red, yellow, and orange).